Life As An Almost

By Vered Hazanchuk

Chapter One: Evie

It isn't raining. I wish it were.

If it were raining, I would think of nothing besides watching the sky open and pour. I would watch the clouds mend themselves into a mouth and say something to me. Anything. I don't want to swim.

Normally, I would love it all. I would love how the other swimmers scribble in the blank space around me and how the water makes the world go quiet. I'd switch it all off—the thoughts, the competition, the whatever—write the judges off and just swim my goddamn hardest. I'd be part of the pack. I'd take it all in. But it's not a good day.

I knew it wouldn't be a good day when I woke up. Everything just felt off. I even sat down and had breakfast, something I haven't done since middle school. But I can be stubborn sometimes. That's what they tell me, Hannah and Mitchell. The people I've lived with the longest. So here I am.

It's almost time to swim. The pool stands empty near a full-length window, lit and smooth, and only slightly bothered by the reflection of a crowd. Now, with ten minutes to kill before the physical fitness portion of the interview, I position myself in a standing lunge to ease the cramping and gently pick away at my name tag, wondering what your name is. What my *real* name is.

Five minutes left. I'm taking deep breaths and counting the tiles on the wall, guessing the depth of the far side of the pool.

Fifty-seven seconds. I'm ready to go. Don't get me wrong. All of me—my mind, my body, all of my insides and out—want to be far, far away from here. But I need to do this swim. And I need to do it well. It's the slow tick of the clock above the pool that's killing me, I decide. The waiting is the worst part of everything, don't you think?

One second left, the whistle blows. We all jump.

The water is lukewarm against my skin. I have on this saggy one-piece that I borrowed from Hannah, because the only swimsuit I own is a yellow bikini with polka-dots that I bought in the beginning of high school, and it didn't seem appropriate for a job interview.

I once hooked up with a guy who told me he recites the beginning of pi in his head when he wants to last longer. Does that work the same for moments, you think? Making them last longer? But I don't have any of pi memorized. I'll settle for what I do know instead: coral is so similar to human bones that it can be used to heal injuries. My bones are not as dense as the woman swimming beside me, with a strong inhale and big curls that keep slipping out of her swim cap. My muscles act a little differently from hers, too. I shouldn't be here. I am here, and I am doing just fine.

Sometimes I wonder what sorts of things I would tell you at the end of the day if you were around, sitting in a small, homey kitchen, dipping freshly made and still melting snickerdoodles into a set of smiley face mugs that I made for us in ceramics class, swinging our feet below the table to the sound of each other's voices. Tonight, I would have come home, thrown my swim bag onto the couch, sat beside you in our living room and told you about this internship in marine conservation biology. That's something I do want, and I need it, too.

When I get out of the water, I duck my head and hope security isn't walking around with headshots of invited participants or something weird like that. The water was nice. Perhaps I did want to swim, after all.

~

She's wearing a matching brown skirt and blazer set, clutching a laptop case with two stickers evenly placed at opposite corners: a heart-shaped one with the Starbucks logo scrawled across it with the added words "Coffee Addict" and one with a camouflage background and a tiny picture of a cabin in the middle, reading "I Survived Lake Tanner Summer Camp." Her sight is focused upward and she's mouthing words as if she's trying to memorize something.

For a moment, her focus breaks and we make eye contact. It's no secret public buses are great for people watching.

There's a shooting pain down my side this afternoon and I'm faking a casual yawn-and-stretch combo to hide it. I'm hiding my medications behind a bent knee, so I don't look like a drug addict or something like that from where I'm wedged in the back of the bus. Twelve more pills. I should have just stopped counting and taken one this morning.

She gives me the up-and-down, smiles, clearly embarrassed, and looks away.

I decide that I don't like her. Is that horrible?

When I imagine you in my head, you look a lot like this girl, with her skinny legs peeking out from a professional façade. How does she get her legs to look smooth? I can never get my razor to do that. With her distant beauty, with her fake survivor sticker.

I'm a real survivor. I know that's not what you meant for and I guess I'm sorry for that.

My name is Evie Mission, I want to say to her. *I have cerebral palsy, and I can swim a 100-meter freestyle in two and a half minutes. I'm getting faster every day. I have a 4.0 GPA. Never mind that I'm not in school right now. I work harder than all those other kids who don't have any college loans to pay off, or even need an internship on their resume at all because their parents "know the right people." I'm determined and I'm passionate. Picturing water as Earth's fluid bones makes me feel calm and safe. And if you don't hire me, you're an idiot*, I add, now picturing the judges I never got to meet today. *You really are.*

Repeating this make-believe confrontation over and over again until I perfect it passes the time until I'm just two stops away. I should have marched in there and really said it, to the backroom past the pool where the judges sit in AC and make small talk with themselves. Then they'd know.

I'm not usually like this, I swear. My heart is still pacing from the thrill of it all, swimming when they told me I couldn't, even beating some of the others, and sneaking out just like that.

It wasn't like me. It was sneaky. It was deceitful. It was instinctive. Is that what survivors act like?

When I was two, my doctor told Hannah, my foster mother, that I was never going to walk. Hannah began to save up for a wheelchair, called the insurance company seeking help paying for ramps, but then I ended up helping myself: I stood.

It was just for a moment, at least the first time. My pudgy little fingers grasped the side of the living room coffee table, throbbed as my two-year-old body sprung upwards, and finally released with one hit to the mouth on the edge of the table and I fell backwards, eyes full of tears. The doctor later called it a cry of celebration. I call it being two years old.

Running my fingers over the opening of the glass window beside me now, bits and pieces of my first memory all come rushing back. The alarming sensitivity forming around my mouth as numbness swelled across my face from the blow, the warm metallic taste of blood oozing from my gums in between the cracks of my teeth, the clamminess beneath my armpits as I was quickly carried from the floor, to the kitchen, to the sink.

They say I'm a survivor. Are survivors supposed to feel like this? To live childhood in and out of surgery when I should have been out trick-or-treating or getting ready for prom, to have the entire local hospital staff know me by name? I don't feel like much of a survivor at all. And with that, I stick my hand outside the window, still clutching my half full bottle of pills, and release.

~

I've always imagined death as some sort of ominous squid, with a capacity for stopping the world. It'd flutter dauntingly around the universe, looking down upon Earth's laborers with the deepest knowledge of all. And with such knowing, death would strike. Suddenly. It'd stifle one last breath out of its victim, steal the color of existence seeping out of a body to paint over the watch of every bystander, cast a spell dismissing all time and place. That's how the world stops; we must stop all together.

But just yesterday I found out that I was wrong about death all along. Death doesn't mean your whole world gets to cave in on you until you can no longer feel the pressing ache of loss and shock sprouting in your chest. It doesn't mean you get to hide underneath your covers and fake ignorance of the world behind your door. Instead, you must crawl out of bed and take your ordinary spot in the ordinary world just like any other ordinary day. It's being gone, and not coming back.

Maybe you won't believe this, but I never truly realized that I myself will die someday. I knew it, of course, but I wasn't spending time sitting around and thinking about it. Not until the day before my internship tryout. It was the day I discovered why I've been having so much trouble getting health insurance that I can actually afford. It's because of you.

I found out by accident. Mitchell and I were the only regulars at Hannah's foster home; the rest of the kids came and went within months, sometimes weeks. Whenever I would wake up in a sweat in the middle of the night from a bad nightmare, Hannah would gently rub my back till I fell back asleep. Whenever I tripped over myself on the school playground, Mitchell would be the one to pull me back up to my feet and walk me to the nurse's office. We have never been a family on paper, but we have always been enough for one another. So when I was told I should probably bring someone with me to my next doctor's appointment in case I wasn't up for driving afterwards, it made sense to ask Hannah to come along.

The doctor's office was a small, windowless room that smelled like bubblegum-flavored cough syrup and rubber gloves. When Hannah offered to go get my refill of pain relievers while we waited, I sat up on the examination table alone and noted how everything in this room was blue. Blue countertops, blue cushioned chairs—I made a game out of it. I smurfed up the entire place in my head.

Blue doctors, blue patients, blue needles that melt to water at the touch of human skin.

But then a couple minutes went by and Hannah still wasn't back. I cracked the door open a bit. Or maybe I was just going to look for a restroom. I don't even remember. But whatever I was looking for, I stopped when I heard the hushed voices of Hannah and a man I didn't recognize.

"We're sorry, ma'am, but her insurance isn't covering the medication. Not anymore."

"There must be some mistake," said Hannah. "She was a child of the state. Doesn't she still get insurance as a student?"

"Not necessarily. Foster care tries to help as much as they can with disabled youth, but now that she's an adult…let's just say finding health insurance with the fees she's used to is going to be tough."

"Because of the cerebral palsy, or…?" The two strangers exchanged a look of understanding.

"Or what?" I asked. I stepped out from the cramped check-up room.

"Evie," said Hannah. "I didn't see you there."

"Or what?" I asked again. "What is it, why won't this man give me my medicine?"

Hannah placed a finger to her chin, the way she does whenever she hesitates. She reached an arm into her purse. Mitchell and I call it her Mary Poppins purse because she always seemed to be carrying around an entire pharmacy in her bag. But this couldn't be solved with a cough drop or a

Band-Aid. Hannah pulled out a file with my name on it.

"You're an adult now," she said. "So, this is yours."

I snatched the file, but I didn't open it.

"Hannah," I started. "Just tell me. Please."

"There's a reason why…you are the way you are. It goes back to your mother." She pointed at the folder. "Your real one."

Chapter Two: Charlotte

It's raining in the middle of the Atlantic tonight, a violent crash of water on water I can never seem to wrap my head around. Both the sun and the moon are absent. I nibble on the mint chocolate placed on my pillow besides the towels, folded, positioned, and styled delicately to make the shape of a bunny rabbit. The housekeepers of the ship like to spoil me.

There's a knock on my cabin door and Kristal, the HR director of the cruise line, pokes her head in.

"Gary wants to have a word," she says.

"I'll be there in just a minute." This seems to satisfy her, and I turn my attention back to my window, a circular and small glimmer of the outside world.

I made sure I was assigned a center room this time, but the rocking of the ship still gets to me every so often, and each swing is followed by the slam and nod of the towel hanger against the wall. The nail it rests upon is loose and unreliable, allowing the cheap, plastic hanger to go about its business running into the wall with every sway of the ship. A constant tap, like a heart monitor. After submitting three work order requests, each gone ignored, I suppose my only options now are to bear the noise or teach myself how to fix it.

But exhaustion gets the best of me most days; I haven't even changed out of my costume yet. Flashy. Sparkly. Short. Disgusting. I was never a huge fan of uniform. With throbbing feet and eye makeup halfway to melting off, I pull a wool sweater over my head and make my way out into the narrow hallway. One of the bulbs hanging from the ceiling flickers, favoring one side of the hall with light over the other.

Don't get me wrong, there is a certain charm to the cruise line lifestyle. After all, nobody out here knows about you. Since my first day here five years ago, nobody has asked much about anything at all. With the exception of Gary. He needs to know everything.

"I called you in here to discuss next season's contract," says Gary. "It's been brought to my attention that you're hesitant to sign."

No hello. No, "How are you doing today?" *I'm quite fine, Gary, thanks for asking, only I'm bored out of my mind here and no one on this entire ship seems to know how to fix a damn shaky hanger when asked politely.*

"Actually, I put in my two weeks' notice this morning." I pause. "Didn't Devin tell you? He told me he did, and said you would probably call me in." Devin is the direct manager of all the servers on the ship. "When we dock back in Miami, my contract is officially over. That will be my last day." Pause. "I really thought you knew, sir. Or else I would have come in here and told you myself."

Gary's overstretched smile looks awkward and completely asymmetrical with the rest of his bulky face. He pulls out a pen from behind his ear and places it before me.

There was one more cruise line before this one—that's where I first met Gary. When he got a new gig five years ago as senior hospitality operations manager, he took me with him. Gave me a number I couldn't refuse and ever since then, this ship has been both of our homes.

Gary was there on my very first day on the cruise job, when I wore the wrong-colored shoes to the opening show staff dance routine all the waiters were required to participate in—white shoes instead of dark brown. We practiced that dance routine for weeks. I ran towards the choreographer with panic bubbling out of me before any sort of words made it out of my mouth, but she didn't want to hear it. She yelled at me to get back in place, the curtains were going up *now*. Goody two-shoes me almost cried.

There was so much freedom then, during my first job away from home. I could stay out of my room as long as I wanted without the nagging responsibility of knowing I should call someone, tell someone where I was. No one cared. I could cry from the relief of it all. But the dance thing—that was one of my first moments when I wished there was someone there to tell me what to do.

Gary saw me, that day with the shoe. "I'm just so embarrassed," I told him after he bought me a drink.

At first, I thought he was hitting on me. Thank God he wasn't because I would have said yes. He was one of the few staff members who wore a suit. We were both babies back then, but being dressed up like that really did make him look older, wiser.

"Thick skin. That's what you're going to need," he said to me. It was simple, but it weirdly stuck. "You're front and center. Pretend it was on purpose. Wear those same shoes to every goddamn routine they put you in from here on out."

Years passed, and I got sick of Gary's need to counsel. He loves being the smart guy, the advice giver. If he could tell the ship why it was floating incorrectly and how thanks to his mathematical expertise and general knowledge of the finest floaters, he knows just what the boat needs to do to make it all better, he would.

His wandering eye doesn't make him the most popular guy on the ship either. Everybody knows he has a wife he hates to talk about.

"Charlotte," Gary starts again, twirling the pen. His eyes settle where they normally do, the sweaty place between my breasts. Doesn't matter that I'm wearing a turtleneck. "I hear you."

I roll my eyes. "Do you, Gary?"

"I've already put in a request with finance to increase your pay—but it's a process. I need you to be patient."

"This really, honestly has nothing to do with money," I start. "Sir, I—"

Gary sighs. "Would you stop calling me sir? I'll tell you what," he says. "Give me an answer by tonight. If not, I'm going to have to give your spot away. Sound good?"

"I really don't need saving, Gary." I breathe, because I've been trying some meditation crap every morning and every night before I go to sleep, and it's supposed to make me not want to tear Gary's head off when he acts pretentious, slimy.

"Well, Jesus Christ, Charlotte. You do this every year, and every year you end up signing, what am I supposed to do? Either you cut the bullshit, or you find another job. I can't keep covering for you. The others would be thrilled to get signed as often as you do."

I want to tell you I have this moment of enlightenment, a sweeping epiphany, but that would just be a lie. I get all haughty, and fed up, and I quit my job. That's the truth.

I stand and say, "Thank you for the opportunity. Sir."

By the time I realize I'm twenty minutes late to one of my last shifts, the thought of speeding up doesn't even cross my mind.

~

Claudia is the only person who seems upset when I announce that I am leaving. A work friend. A waitress, like me.

Claudia was from the Philippines and planning on studying accounting in America before she had her daughter and landed this job away from her family eleven months a year. *For a better life*, she would always say to me five minutes before our night shifts ended, when the moonlight was at its brightest, and the hour at its loneliest, and the locket with the picture of her daughter, now nine years old, pressed against her palm.

The day after my meeting with Gary, Devin very forcefully suggested I leave as soon as we are on land, at our next stop, three days away, instead of waiting until we're back in Miami. *Optional personal time*, they call it.

"I know it's not how it's usually done, but I'm not going to fight," I say to Claudia with a shrug. "If they really want me gone that badly, I'll take the hint."

"They're being ridiculous," she says with an eyeroll, scrubbing the counters as we talk. "When was the last time you were home?" Claudia asks.

I pause. "Years and years ago? I honestly can't even remember."

Dad's funeral was brief and back where he grew up in Utah, on the same patch of land his side of the family has buried each other in for decades. The opportunity to skip the homecoming was welcomed.

"It will be weird being home after all this time, that's for sure," I add.

Claudia shakes her head. "Don't forget about us little people. When you're back to your glamorous Californian life."

"I'm just seeing my mother for a bit," I say. "Not running off to Hollywood or something. I probably won't even stay."

"Where will you go?" she asks.

"No idea," I say. "I haven't thought that far ahead yet. But we'll still see each other again soon, I'm sure of it."

I know I've burned a bridge here with management. It's become personal, the sudden leave. Another cruise line? The thought makes me a little sad. But it's what I know. A long time ago, I thought I might be a lawyer someday.

People tend to stick around at cruise jobs. It takes a certain type of person to live at sea, and once you've conformed, you just stay.

Claudia's smirking at me.

"What?" I ask.

"Trust me," says Claudia. "You're never coming back."

~

I was fifteen. Keith was seventeen. We were walking around the park nearest to my house and arguing about the correct lyrics to the *Prince of Bel-Air* theme song, or something completely irrelevant like that.

"It's 'It had dice in the mirror.' I'm positive," I said.

"Nope. It's 'I looked twice in the mirror.' *I'm* positive."

"Dice."

"Twice."

"Dice!" I pushed him and he faked a fall, pulling me down with him. Sitting up in his lap, I nudged him as I giggled. "Get up!"

He leaned into me so that our foreheads touched and eyes met for just a moment before he kissed me. His lips were full and soft against mine as he parted my lips with his tongue and slipped into my mouth. And then we were shifting bodies, and rolling over each other, and panting into the grass, and crashing kisses into each other.

His hand shot up my skirt, fumbling at the elastic lining of my underwear. A twinge of shock sprouted up in between my thighs as the tip of his finger stroked my uncovered skin. I got a hold of his wrist and began to push him away, but he tensed. "Keith…"

He breathed heavily into my ear and spoke in a whimper. "Please?" I shook my head slowly. He wet his lips and drew in closer to me. "Please. C'mon." Each word felt lighter than the one before in the dense air. "I really," he said as he pecked my lips. "Really." Peck. "Want you."

And because he was already nearly inside of me and it was all so easy, I didn't say no again. All it took was a nod for us to make love that night. Fast, mindless love. And after the first time, well, hell, nothing else seemed to matter so much anymore.

What I remember most about our relationship, the relationship that seemed like the most important thing in the world at the time, doesn't have to do with the two of us at all. It's not a memory the two of us shared, or a fight we had, or even that first night together. What I remember most is late nights, alone, wanting to touch his body so badly, wanting to be held and kissed, and then the disappointment washing over me when all I felt was numb in his arms. Every single night we spent together, I would press myself closer and closer against his chest and wonder why I still felt so empty.

Chapter Three: Evie

The best part about living in Half Moon Bay is an abandoned wooden pier at the very end of Main Street. It's around the corner of some clothing boutiques and seafood restaurants, and it still carries the remnants of a time when it was something big— feel-good-music on repeat, pastel-colored skies, rows of wooden coffee shops, and surfers streaming in from downtown. Now it echoes empty sounds of strong wind currents and faraway laughter.

There's a strip of sand beneath the rolling hills of yellow bushes and weeds leading up to the pier's narrow mouth, always smelling of sea salt mixed with wet dirt. If you can stand the rough patches of chipped wood and soil beneath your bare toes, you can see past the mist, straight to the end of the pier where I like to dangle my feet over the edge and just be. It's my favorite place in the world.

A few times a year, usually during the winter when everyone was preparing for the holidays and it was too cold for locals to devote much time to the beach anyways, Hannah would get one of the other bus drivers to double up on stops for the day and she'd take Mitchell and me to the end of Main Street. *Just this one day*, she would always say.

We'd spend hours walking on the shore, picking seashells and trying to skip rocks; the waves would be too fast, but we would keep staring out at the sea, wondering if the glimmer across the way was really just foam or if it was finally our rock taking a leap.

The best moments happened to me by the pier. There, I could study the little tide pool to the left and still keep an eye out for the rocks. I would scoop the algae out of the water and admire the slimy feel of it in between my fingers.

A visit during third grade was the best. I threw my brackets away two years before then, my limp improved, and I became strong enough to walk for about thirty minutes before having to rest. I remember dipping my big toe in the cold water, then all five toes, then my entire foot. I felt Mitchell watching me and looked up at him, mind already set. He seemed to shake his head with his eyes in the slow second before I jumped in. My first swim.

Now Mitchell walks beside me on the dry, cold sand and says the same thing he said to me when I got into the water that day: "Stop trying to be brave."

"Believe me," I answer this time. "That's the last thing I'm trying to be."

Mitchell cocks one of his thick eyebrows at me. His lips are pressed tightly together like he always does when he's trying to be serious, yet the pressing fails, as always, to conceal his distinct dimples. I wonder how Mitchell would be as a father, unable to keep a steady sternness for two minutes.

"So, what are you going to do?"

"Get a job, I guess," I answer. "What other choice do I have?"

Mitchell glances at me, nods, and doesn't say anything for a while.

Twenty years old and I've already dropped out of college a bunch of times to work the fast-food drive-throughs and tutor high school kids. But for some reason I keep coming back, and so do my medical bills. I've dodged copay for as long as possible. I'm a home remedies expert for nearly everything in the book. But there are some things magnesium supplements and lemon water can't fix. And out-of-pocket costs for painkillers or muscle relaxants are a whole different story.

"Not to rush you, but you know rent is due," he finally says.

"Ugh. Cover me?"

"Always."

"Sorry," I say.

"No worries. If you're serious about taking on a full-time job, though, someone from my gym works at a daycare. Said she's looking for some help."

"Kids?"

"Yeah, why not?" asks Mitchell.

"I don't know how."

A single *hah* falls out of Mitchell's lips. "Know how to *what?*" he asks.

"I don't know. Know what to do with them," I say. "I don't know the first thing about kids."

"Honestly, Evie," he says. "As long as they're safe and happy by the end of the day when their parents come to pick them up, you're good. It's just temporary, right?"

"Yeah. Okay, fine. I guess I'll look into it."

We walk in silence for a while. "Still, a bummer though, huh?" Mitchell says quietly.

"What? Oh, that." I shrug. "It's whatever." Pause, pause, should I do it? Should I say it? "I wasn't allowed to try out." This single truth gushes out of me like a dirty secret.

"What do you mean?" asks Mitchell.

I hand him the crumpled email print-out I've been carrying around for weeks in my back pocket, sticking out of my purse, shuffled between my hands as I reread and reread. I've been carrying it around in all of these places, always somehow touching me. A reminder.

Mitchell takes a while with the letter and his eyebrows scrunch as he reads. "Fuck them," is what he eventually says, handing me back the piece of paper a bit more crumpled than when I gave it to him.

We keep walking. The tide is fairly low today, and quiet. If I don't look to our right, I can almost forget where we are. There are so many ways for an ocean to sound. It can whisper, or hiss, or roar. It's protective. Fish and other cold-blooded sea animals rely on specific heat to regulate their own body temperatures. Specific heat. Extreme rises or extreme drops wouldn't cut it. So even if the outside world is rough, and drops ten or twenty degrees by nightfall, and sends harsh winds that knock over sailboats and other human things—water absorbs the heat from the sun during the day, holds on to it, and then slowly releases it bit by bit so that water temperature doesn't change much. It's just right.

"They can't do that," grumbles Mitchell. He's still talking about the email, from the internship. He's looking straight ahead, at a French bulldog on the beach rubbing his back on the sand. He prefers bigger dogs. *More to love*, he always says, when we pretend that we'll get a dog together one day.

"Let it go, Mitch," I say. And he does.

I still haven't been completely honest with Mitchell. I haven't told him about what happened after try-outs, at the doctor's office. I'm too tired. I'm too confused. I'm waiting for Hannah to. I'm waiting for specific heat. Mitchell makes things real. What does that make me?

When it starts to get dark out, we walk back to Mitchell's Nissan Altima parked nearby and drive home. I take a three-hour nap, even though I'm not very tired. I feel safe here, sinking in between the cracks of the exhausted couch cushions and the sight of too many cars crammed together during rush hour at a far distance outside our living room window.

Most of our furniture, including all the chairs and the dining room table, are mismatched foldables. The only spot of color are some velvet blue curtains that came with the place when we first moved in, abandoned by the tenants before us. They are long, formless, and so much larger than the window itself that they restrict most light from coming in at all.

It occurred to me once that we could just take them down. Yet they've been here longer than I have and have seen dozens moving in and out, so I decided that until we get some acceptable decorations for our place, I am a guest and the curtains stay where they belong. But it's been two years at this place and it still looks like we're camping. On our way out. Old habits of us fosters, I guess.

I wake up to Mitchell using the blender. He thinks I can't hear because there's a wall separating our living room from our kitchen. I can totally hear.

"Mitchell." Bzzzz. "Mitch." Bzzzz! "Mitchell!"

He stops the blender. "Did you say something?"

"I'm trying to sleep." I place a pillow over my face. "Sorry to *bother* you."

He laughs, pours himself a glass of the smoothie, pushes my feet off the couch and sits down.

Somewhere in between the stitches of our fractured childhood, Mitchell figured life out. His world became simple when his parents died; Mitch always says *simple, as in, not much*, with laughing eyes and deep dimples.

News of the car crash came to him in the middle of a game of hide-and-seek, four-year-old him peeping out from the hallway coat closet and his nanny standing in the doorway with a police officer and a state counselor, horror written across her body as she walked backwards to Mitchell's bedroom and packed him a duffle bag for his first night away.

Then there were a few very short and formal stays, mostly a week or two at a time. Mitch says he doesn't remember any of them. I don't know if that's true, but I do know how irrelevant all those misfit homes became when he was finally placed at 667 East Merry Way, Hannah's home. He stayed with her until he turned eighteen and packed his bag for college. So did I.

Which is in itself a miracle, really, because only about ten percent of foster kids go to college. Mitch says it's because Hannah always talked about how much her father wanted to go to college. About how much reading books can change someone's life. The American dream. How Hannah wasn't very strict, but how crystal clear she made it that going to school every single day and getting there on time, every time, was a requirement. *Think of it as rent for kids*. Mitchell always says it's because of Hannah. I think my college career is ninety percent little Evie wanting to be just like Mitchell. Just don't tell him that.

Hannah didn't have a lot of money. She never did and still doesn't, but she was enough. She was a single, middle-aged woman who emigrated from Ukraine as a teenager with her elderly father in search of an easier, American life and a new beginning after her mother died from stomach cancer. She just barely made rent every month, but always did her best to be on time. Since no one wants to adopt a kid old enough to walk, and talk, and remember, she got Mitchell.

We both got lucky, we always remind each other. We weren't stuck in a big group home, which can be swamped with children—four, five, six to a room. If there isn't enough space, they'll have kids sleep in the offices of social workers sometimes. Sleeping bags, the nightshift checking in on them every once in a while, telling them they need to go to bed already.

At 667 East Merry Way, there were two bedrooms for children to sleep in. Two bunk beds, one faded bean bag in the corner, white walls plastered with photos of forest animals cut out from *National Wildlife*, and a giant world map held up with blue painter's tape was the boys' room, or Mitchell's room plus guests.

My room was much smaller, yet charming. Full of old, battered things. Washed-out, yellow floral wallpaper with white trimming, a wooden toy box from a garage sale we accidentally passed by years ago, quilts of pale pinks and greens draped around nearly every piece of furniture because I was the kind of child that was always cold.

Cinnamon on a low simmer floating off the stove top for a homey smell. We were mostly a pasta household, but sometimes Hannah would let us watch her make something special—sausages and other meats, artichokes dressed in olive oil and lemon juice, or goat cheese sprinkled on anything that sounded good at the beginning of the month when the state paid child support. I spent most of my time indoors. It was a peculiar but gentle sort of childhood.

I'll admit that I used to wonder about you. Unlike Mitchell, I had no idea where I came from and I never really questioned why not. At least not aloud. Every once in a while, I'd think, *hey, isn't it strange? Isn't it funny how I have no idea who you are, or where you are, or why you gave me up*, and at the latest hours of the night when the wind wailed and slammed itself against my bedroom window, my tiny fists hurting as the air lessened from my pulling the blanket around me extra tight, I'd imagine you never gave me up at all. That some horrible creature, a monster like the one some kids thought lived under the bed, went around stealing children from their parents late at night and left them scattered about the streets for the state to find. You had soft curls down to your shoulders of light brown, like mine, and smelled of vanilla extract and honey. You used coconut oil on your face and lips because your skin was sensitive and dried in the sun. You folded clothes before putting it in the wash because that's proper and comforting and clothes should always be folded. You had a sweet tooth and snuck in bites of peanut butter cookies while cooking dinner and believed no meal was complete without homemade dessert. Your voice was tender, but your laugh was thunder—I knew that woman so well, I swear it.

As the night nears midnight and I still find myself sitting with nothing but my thoughts on the couch, *Full House* reruns going in the background, I seriously consider burning the file from Hannah's

Mary Poppin's bag. But with the start of tomorrow, I decide against it.

Chapter Four: Charlotte

"We've lost touch," is the best I could come up with when Kristal appeared at my door, again, claiming that my mother keeps emailing the front desk asking for a way to reach me. That my mother says she's sorry to disturb, but this is the only way she could think of to contact me in time. That she is moving out of my childhood home by the end of the month and needs help packing up "all of this junk" *immediately.* Lord, I hope the woman that raised you has more sense than mine does.

"None of my business, ma'am," said Kristal with both eyebrows raised, wrinkling her forehead. This was just a day before I quit. I guess I wasn't just fed up with Gary looking down my shirt, making sly remarks. I guess I was thinking about my mother.

After Kristal's visit, I consider my options.

Option one: pray.

But it's been so long, I'm afraid I won't do it right. The first thing I did when I found out about you, twenty years ago, was pray.

It was homecoming week. There were brightly colored everything: fundraiser stands beside the field selling all sorts of snacks and hot drinks, red ribbons on the bleachers, yellow streamers everywhere, newly plastered banners parading in the wind and carrying the sweet smell of freshly cut grass with them.

In high school, I was the painfully shy one. I never liked that about myself. Somewhat desperately, I tried to change. Every school dance, every rally, every football game, every club meeting; I forced myself to be everywhere. And yet, no matter where I went, the familiar grip of speechlessness would be waiting for me in the middle of a crowd, every time. It choked me.

Cruise life, it turns out, was the real cure for my shyness. There's something about the middle of the ocean that makes us all a little lonely. And then, a little chatty.

My parents hated the shyness about me, too; I could tell. So much so that I even considered asking them for a ride to the homecoming game that night, just to show them that I was trying. But I knew they would never approve of this particular plan. Nothing good came of late Friday nights, according to them, and I was out past my curfew.

My latest project, three girls I knew from church, were going. I couldn't risk the parents saying no. So I decided to follow my usual escape route, an early bedtime excuse and crawling out the window.

That's not to say these girls were my friends. Becky, Viola, and Rachel, the three of them were friends. Best friends. I was tolerated. I waited for conversational clues when we were together about where they were meeting up next and I'd force myself to consider it an invitation.

As for real friends, I didn't have any. Not really. I was pretty used to being alone, only child and all. I was lucky that Keith chose me. He was older and graduated two years before this, class of '90. And ever since, I'd been not only painfully shy at school, but painfully alone.

Don't feel sad for me about all this. Despite my efforts, I actually didn't mind being the loner type sometimes. Besides, the Becky-Viola-Rachel trio were pretty girls and I liked being around them. Delicately dressed, high cheekbones, soft smiles. I collected the precious moments when I felt like one of them.

As we walked and ate kettle corn together around the school—close enough to the football field that we vaguely knew what was going on, far enough that we didn't have to concern ourselves with the score—I tried my best to make sense of the boys the girls talked about. Boys I couldn't place because they used nicknames for each of them. A code system made up to keep the boys clueless, I was sure.

"Look!" Viola said suddenly. "There's Sam." A real name. I knew this one.

"He's coming this way," whispered Rachel.

"Well, duh, he is. I told him we'd be here," said Becky.

Sam smiled. "What's up, ladies?"

"Hey, Sam," said Becky. "What's up? Where are the guys?"

"They're waiting for us out back," he told us, nodding toward the school pool entrance. Sam was one of the student lifeguards. I'm pretty sure that's the only reason Viola and Rachel joined the water polo team.

"Sweet. Let's go then," said Becky and grinned at us girls.

We followed Sam to the back gate. *You're welcome*, Becky's eyes were saying. Sam unlocked the back gate and let us scurry in before him. There were loud whispers above us. We all looked up where the boys' feet dangled above us. They were seated on the roof of the small lifeguard tower. Sam leaned his heels against the side of the fence and swung himself upwards in one swift movement. Then he reached his arm out and pulled us up one by one.

"Coast is clear?" asked one of Sam's friends.

"Coast is clear," answered Sam. They pulled out some beer cans from a blue, worn-out Jansport backpack and began to pass them around. We must have all leaned away at the same time because Becky shot us a quick, annoyed look. "What's the matter with you guys?" she whispered hotly.

"Becky, you don't drink," said Viola.

"None of us do," said Rachel.

Becky popped the can open and took a quick sip. "I do now." She offered her beer over to us, but none of us moved.

"Hey, Duncan! I dare you to jump into the pool from here," said Sam, looking down over the rooftop. The rest of the guys snickered. I would have looked over the side of the roof, too, but I knew we were high enough for me to get dizzy. I was never very good with heights. The jump would have been brutal.

Duncan laughed, hopped up onto his feet and began to peel his shirt off for the leap. This really got the guys going. They kept clapping and hollering the closer Duncan got to the edge.

"Are you crazy? You're going to hurt yourself," I said, and I could feel the other girls nodding silently behind me.

"Aw, come on, ladies." Duncan grabbed a beer and held it out towards me. "Live a little."

When I didn't make a move for it, he went for my purse. "Fine. Take one for the road."

"Don't!" I instinctively grabbed the purse and held it tight to my chest. Blushing, I realize how loud my voice was. I didn't mean to yell.

"Take a chill pill," someone murmured. Aside from that and a few weird glances, they left me alone. I peeped inside of the purse, spotted the still unopened pregnancy test I bought after school, grabbed Becky's drink, and had my first big gulp of alcohol.

When the adult voices drifted up to our hideout, we naturally scattered. The boys all jumped up and off the rooftop in lightning speed. I somehow managed to slip back down to the ground without too many bruises and run out the gate towards the street.

From there, I walked the rest of the two blocks to my house slowly. The window creaked as I gently pushed it shut behind me, still crouched on my bedroom desk from the climb, but it ended up not mattering. My dad was in the shower and my mother was fast asleep.

My childhood twin bed had a stiffness to it whenever I got underneath the covers. Maybe it was stuck in a time when my parents tucked me in too tight for comfort. I'd usually toss and turn for at least an hour until I found that one sweet spot and finally allowed myself to surrender to drowsiness.

But that night, I struggled in between heavy blinks and drawn-out yawns to stay up long enough to say my prayers. I prayed you were just a dream. And I guess I got it, for the past few years that's all you really were.

~

Option two: run.

When I walked down the stairs and into the kitchen that morning after homecoming, a bowl of oatmeal and a fruit cup were shoved at me and I was told to eat quickly, but healthy and chew well. We didn't want to be late to the SATs.

My stomach gave an uneasy churn as I stirred the soggy oats in my bowl around with a spoon. My dad, an orthodontist, was called into the office early that morning to fix a poking wire, so I only had my mother there with me at the kitchen table. She pulled out the stack of vocabulary flashcards and tested me in between bites. I jabbed each oat in the middle and watched as it flexed and floated back up to the surface instead of splitting into two. When I forgot to answer her trivia completely, she plopped the flashcards down and stared at me.

"Charlotte," she said. "Are you even paying attention?"

I glanced at her and nodded slightly.

"What's wrong, honey, don't you feel good?" She put a hand to my forehead.

I hesitated. "Just nervous, I guess."

"Oh, sweetie, you'll be fine. We've studied so much," she said as she glanced at her watch and helped me pull my backpack onto my shoulders. She kissed my forehead and saw me out the door.

Morning walks were usually my favorite. I loved how there was nothing to listen to but the buzz of faraway airplanes and the lighthearted tap of shoe soles against pavement. Time passed more slowly and the sky stretched longer than usual. Whiffs of strong coffee would sometimes leak out when the neighbors left their kitchen windows open, my favorite. My parents tried their best to steer me away from caffeine and too much sugar, so the only morning drinks we'd have at home were low-fat milk and natural orange juice.

But today was different. Everything was abnormally still. My steps boomed in the screaming silence. I considered going to the mall instead, wondering if I'd be the first honor student ever to play hooky on SAT day, but I knew I never really would. I just couldn't.

I dragged myself into my assigned room where fifteen or so other students were already sitting and waiting to begin. Instead of cramming, I went through the mental checklist in my head that I'd rehearsed a dozen times a day during test prep:

Three sharpened number two pencils—check.
Approved scientific calculator—check.
Reading glasses—check.
Pink elastic eraser—check.

Then the instructor stood before us and mumbled a couple things about integrity and testing procedure. She passed out the test booklets. That's when I realized that funny feeling I woke up with was more than just nerves. I held on with both hands to the edge of my desk. She was nearing my table. She placed my copy of the SATs in front of me, and then I vomited all over it.

~

The school nurse eventually caught up to me and dragged me back to her office after I ran out of the classroom, all scarlet-faced and hot. She handed me two paper towels, one damp and one dry, and instructed me to clean myself up. I let my head rest back against the matted chair as she took my temperature.

She said she couldn't find anything wrong with me and began filling out a health report for my parents, who were already on their way. She asked me if I took any medications. She asked me about any allergies I may have. She asked me when my last period was, and I told her the truth.

The nurse blinked at me a couple of times, but said nothing. She was a wrinkled woman, with long yellow hair she tied back into a low ponytail with a thick white scrunchie. Her eyes were a clear blue and she wore no makeup, which shrank her little eyelids deeper into her face. When we heard the front door crack open, we waited for one another to offer some sort of reaction. I stared back at her. She stood and walked over to where my parents rushed in.

So that's how they found out about you.

I glued my eyes downwards on the blue rug beneath my feet as she explained the vomit, the weight increase, everything that was wrong with me. She said teen pregnancy was more common these days. She said that these things happen.

At first, I wasn't sure what to expect from them. They were quiet, which scared me. They always had some sort of tidbit to offer, a statistic to recite that they had just read in the paper. Today they seemed just as confused as I was. We walked back home together but hardly noticed each other as we each creased our forehead in thought, a collective family habit of ours.

My mom unlocked the door, tossed her bag down on the beige leather couch, and locked herself away in the master bathroom for an hour and a half. My dad, on the other hand, paced around the entire house. I found him finally taking a breather in the kitchen, with both his hands leaning against the counter and his head drooping.

"Dad?" He seemed surprised to see me.

"Just go to bed, Charlotte," he said quietly. "We'll deal with this tomorrow."

~

Option three: go home. Can't say I can really relate a story to this one. So I buy a ticket for the next plane ride to San Jose, California and wait.

Chapter Five: Evie

I met plenty of kids who got a rush from it—shoplifting. *It's such a rush,* they'd all say, *when you get away with it.*

One girl told me she never actually wore any of the things that she stole. Most everyone else I knew didn't care—clothes, toys, snacks, gadgets, whatever. They used it all.

I only did it because I was hungry. I hadn't eaten something with real nutrients in it in four days. Nothing warm in nine, and my entire body was driving me crazy. It was hard to think about much of anything else.

So, I stole. It's not like I haven't done it before. I once stole a book about global myths and beliefs from the public library that said spitting cleanses the body of evil.

I spit three times onto the sidewalk, find an empty park bench, and sit with my medium pepperoni and mushroom pizza, extra mushrooms. The take-out slip taped to the front of the cardboard box says it was meant for someone named Tori.

I inhale the first slice. I don't remember the second. I start to feel guilty by the third. The fourth dyes my hands with its oozing red sauce and the fifth puts me in the mood for sharing.

Mitchell works at an auto body shop two blocks away. The place smells of oil and the stale odor of a day's worth of sweat. Mitch sees me right as I walk in and nods in greeting.

"Special delivery," I say and hold the mostly eaten pizza out to Mitch.

"What's this?"

I shrug. "Just thought I'd say hello."

"What's your deal? You've been in an extra bad mood lately. And it's lasted longer than a week so don't try to use that excuse." When I stare at him blankly, he adds, "Period?"

"I'm truly shocked that you're still single," I respond.

I thought he'd laugh, at least roll his eyes. He doesn't. Instead he gets us both drinks from the minifridge and says, "Are we going to talk about that email?"

I don't respond.

"From those bastards saying you failed the physical before you even tried out?" Mitchell continues, as if I don't remember. "Could they have at least waited until after tryouts? Automatic fail— bullshit."

"Forget the email, Mitchell. I asked you to. Remember?"

He shakes his head. "I just can't believe it."

"It's fine, Mitch."

"Like some kind of liability. Couldn't even personalize the email. It was obviously a template."

"Mitchell. I know."

"Needing a doctor's note. Can't believe that's what did it. A prerequisite or whatever, I guess, but why even hold tryouts in the first place, if you're going to base your entire decision off a doctor's note, am I right? We all know you can swim faster than all of those assholes."

"I definitely cannot outswim most of those kids, Mitch, but okay—"

"And does it really matter how fast you are? It's not like you're racing. You're not trying out for the Olympics—"

"Mitchell!"

"What?" He looks confused.

"You know what I'd love? To talk about literally anything. Anything at all, besides this." I feel the back of my neck get red. Mitchell looks away and starts trying to crack his knuckles.

I know what he's thinking about. He's thinking about you. He'll keep thinking about you until he gets another chance to throw all of his untamed thoughts at me.

I look around the body shop and peek behind the front door. The cubbies inside the small office where the staff keep their stuff is always a disaster of unzipped jackets and stale food, but the rest of the room is tidy, smelling of the pine scent plug-in Mitchell's boss always insists on. "It's always so calm in here," I say. *Why, oh why, can't I be more like Mitchell?*

The funny thing is, I know that he thinks I'm the one who is making it somehow, the one who has got it together. The dream, the ambition, the drive, the whatever else people only describe each other as.

"So." Mitchell clears his throat. "Heard you got the job with Alice. Congrats. When do you start?"

"That's what I wanted to ask you actually. She emailed me back and said I could start at the end of the month, but I can't wait that long. I want to start right away. Could you get me her direct cell number? I tried her office line a couple times, but she never answers."

"Of course."

"Thanks," I say.

"I know asking if you're excited would be outrageous," starts Mitchell. I glare. "Are you at least looking forward to it? Something new."

"I need cash," I respond in between gulps of beer.

"I think working with Alice will be good for you," he says. "She's all about analyzing dreams and transformative meditation and stuff. Mid-, late-, early-life crises. She likes helping people like you."

I snort. "Please. Most people don't even know people like me are alive."

Now Mitchell glares. "Horrible choice of words."

~

She's one of those people who decorate the place with Christmas lights all year round, with the calculated looping strings tangled around the rim, and symmetric colored bulbs, and all. She's hovering over the side balcony, reaching over the edge to peer at something in the parking lot that caught her attention.

After I knock on the open door for a second time, she finally sees me and prances over. She talks, and talks, and hands me a schedule of daily activities and a list of daycare rules. Says she's excited to work with me, and to ask if I have any questions or problems while on the job, and that the kids are so great and so excited to meet me. She then points out every child in the room to me individually and lists all of their food allergies. I nod, and nod, and nod.

It turns into a long day. A long, long day.

It all begins with me not cutting up the snacks right. I cut the apples into slices, when really, they are supposed to be cut into squares so they can be mixed in with the blueberries and strawberries. The mini fruit salad is always placed in the blue paper cups that I forgot to get from the cupboard, so I use paper bowls instead, which are supposed to be used for lunchtime only, not snack time.

Then it's naptime, and I help one girl roll out her sleeping mat, but place it wrong side up, so she starts crying, and I ask her what's wrong but she's too sniffly and snotty and weepy to answer so I just keep asking her, which I guess isn't the right thing to do because I swear I see Alice roll her eyes— she's capable of doing that?—before she sits down, and flips the sleeping mat right side up, and talks the girl into settling in.

After nap time, I get the kids in line and lead them to the playground, and on the way, I accidentally slap a kid in the face when quickly lifting my hand to swat a fly away from me. I hit a damn kid in the face, what is wrong with me?

In my defense, his face is right fucking there. I mean, how else am I supposed to lift my hand besides up? His face just happens to be at the same level.

So of course he starts crying, too. That brings the number of children that have cried today because of me up to two. And every time I mess up, Alice smiles at me kindly, slowly, and says in a particularly high voice, "No worries, no worries."

She keeps finding new things for me to do. Eventually she tells me to work with Harold, who she doesn't like to leave unentertained for too long. He is sitting by himself by the Legos.

So I start playing with this kid. I'm not going to put it lightly. Harold drives me crazy. He pees on the floor nearly every time he feels the need to instead of asking to use the restroom, and is constantly running in sloppy circles, throwing his head around from side to side and rolling his eyes back like a possessed munchkin. I hear from one of the other kids that he tried to throw a rock at an assistant's head once, and was much too close to succeeding for a kid who can't even reach the bathroom sink yet, and when I drag him in jagged lines to his seat for a timeout after acting up, he begins throwing his fists into the air like a raver. When I tell him to stop, he gets all pissed off and says, "Batman didn't have to stop."

I tell him he isn't Batman. Never EVER tell a five-year-old boy that he isn't Batman.

He starts screaming, and then all the kids at his table start screaming, and a couple of boys start laughing, and one of them starts crying, and Alice comes in and yells at them for me because I can't do it right.

Believe me, I try. I do the whole wide-eyed look-at-me-when-I'm-trying-to-be-angry-with-you thing, and the strong evil voice, and the low scary tone when that doesn't work. None of it seems to change anything.

When it is finally time to go home, I'm exhausted. I fold up my green zip-up sweatshirt to slip into my purse with my sunglasses and new staff badge. Alice floats over to the coat hanger next to my things where her purse dangles and gives me a big grin. I wait for her constructive criticism. I practically beg her for it with my eyes, to no avail. She doesn't even seem to be thinking about anything that happened earlier today.

"Great day today, Evie," is all she says. "See you tomorrow!"

~

"So. What'd you think?"

"She's too perky."

"Well. Yeah." Mitchell rolls his eyes. "I meant the job. How was it?"

"Meh," I answer.

"Meh?"

"It's a job," I say. "You said it yourself, just another temporary gig to save up for classes. And then there will probably be another. And another."

"Negative Nancy over here."

"I prefer Realistic Rachel," I respond.

"Just as long as you don't get started with the sob stories," says Mitchell.

I blink at him.

"Pity me, I'm so poor." Fists rubbing his dry eyes complete his fake cry. "You're stronger than that," says Mitch.

"Can't I be strong *and* negative?"

"I thought you called that whining realistic."

I'm the one to roll my eyes this time.

~

The next gig for me tonight is at a take-out sushi place. It's afterhours, which is a convenient way to balance the two jobs, mopping the floors and getting the place cleaned up, sometimes taking stock of supplies so the cook and the rest of the morning crew can start as soon as they get in early the next morning.

I wonder, briefly, if I can squeeze a third job in there. Only temporarily. It'd be nice not to have to worry about extra spending money. And who knows, maybe I'll even be able to get back to school by the next semester.

The irony here is that I fall asleep only shortly after this genius idea of mine. Three jobs. Hah.

I didn't get caught or anything. I took a seat at one of the plastic booths—do they even try to make these things comfortable?—and I was out as soon as my arm hit the tabletop, forehead hit my arm.

No one is in the room with me to see, but I wake up blushing. Someone, probably my boss or one of his kids, opens and closes a few of the kitchen cabinets. I can hear them tip over something as they lean in to reach for whatever it is that they're looking for.

It is usually just me and the family who owns the restaurant during my shift. They used to clean it all themselves, they told me, but they could use the help. *To get out early*, they kept saying during the quick interview we had last week when I first saw the "Help Wanted" sign in the window. I started the job within a day.

They haven't left early at all since I've started. I don't mind, it being my first few days and all. And, admittedly, I think I have a crush on this family.

It's not much, but I love the mother's voice. I love the father's playfulness, always grabbing the youngest—he's eight—and lifting him slowly, as if he's super heavy, before throwing him up in the air, tousling his hair, pulling the hood of his sweatshirt over his eyes.

The boy, in contrast to his father, is so serious. He's always calling his father "too silly." I see him secretly grin every time he gets thrown up in the air or a hood thrown over his face. He's small for his age.

The teenage daughter is quiet and usually handles washing the dishes. They seem easygoing, and I like that.

I'm particularly thankful for the little boy's shrieking laugh today, which snaps me out of my drowsy state. I'm still sitting, and decide I should probably get up and look busy.

I revisit the mop I propped up against the wall and note a concert must have just ended as I glance out the window. There's a large show venue just down the street. The generally empty sidewalk fills with clusters of people.

I had a dream just now, while snoozing on the job, and it was kind of like that. The sudden buzzing of leftover energy on a deserted street—a comparison, an opposite, a confusion. You were there, and so was I. I didn't see either of us, but somehow, I knew we were there—both of us. Do you ever have those kinds of dreams, where you don't see anything right, but you just know?

What I did see were tree branches. Lots of them, all over the place. Thick wooden arms twisted, wrapped around each other. They looked strong, but if you stared for too long, they would soften. Fall into a heap of spaghetti. Fall away into a groundless place at the bottom of my dream world. I didn't want to touch them, to make them turn into jelly, but I couldn't stop.

It's a stupid dream, but I wake up sweaty just the same.

I wonder what Alice would have thought of it.

When I was younger, it was different. I didn't know any better. A mother, any plain old mother, that's what I wanted. But now, all I'd like is to stop thinking about you. *A quiet life*, that's what the owner of the restaurant told me he was always after. It was my first time meeting him, that day he casually said this to me with a goofy grin on his face as he interviewed me for the job. Immediately, I decided that I liked him.

We quit our corporate jobs to open this place up, he said proudly as he knocked on the wall behind him. We stood across from each other in the back room between the storage shelves and the small desk shoved in the corner. The place had framed black and white photos of local beaches on the walls.

For a quieter life, he said, when he told me how long he and his wife dreamed of going into the food business together. *For a quieter life*, he said, when he told me how he wants his kids to keep working here until college. They'll make decisions better, then, after helping the family business. So much care, care for the details of the lives that will carry on beyond his time. This is what made me feel that he was a good man, my new boss.

I sigh loudly at my mop. The teenage girl stares at me. "Are you okay?" she asks.

I give her a toothy smile. She blinks and turns her attention back to the binder she came in here for. After finding it on the front counter, she returns to her family in the back room.

Quiet, I realize, is just another word for ordinary to this family. Peaceful. I think I'd like a quieter life.

Chapter Six: Charlotte

I was at ten weeks when I first seriously realized that there were options besides the ones my parents had laid out for me. The "A" word, among others, was not allowed in my childhood home.

Pamphlets and Planned Parenthood advertisements on the radio. That's when it all began unraveling in my head. The truth, that is. Could I really go to college someplace besides BYU, or study abroad in Paris, or take a year off to save up and move to someplace far from the suburbs, far from home? Could I erase a mistake, and be forgiven? I couldn't get the damn thoughts to stop. It was scary and it was absolutely liberating.

I ditched math class and walked to the nearest clinic by my school. I lied and told them that I didn't have health insurance, then paid in cash with all the money I saved up from three years of babysitting.

I remember:

Machines humming in the waiting room. It sounded like an airplane about to take off.

Magazine covers without images, just words. *Health, Women's Fitness, Food & Travel.*

Being unable to curl my body into a comfortable position on the hospital bed they left me on.

The smell of rubber and faint leftovers of a citrus cleaning wipe.

Squirming on top of the fresh folds of the paper bed cover, creating tiny crinkles.

Watching the clock.

Hearing my breath bounce off the pale blue walls.

Jumping as the doctor opened the door in one swift moment.

How cold the room got just then.

Lifting my paper gown, exposing my purple floral underwear with the yellow bow on the top, crossing my legs and letting my head drop to the left.

Blinking at the monitor.

The chill of the jelly squeezed from a long, colorless tube onto my stomach, the ultrasound probe running and pressing at my skin.

Listening to the quietness, and then listening to you.

Thinking of string.

I cried for an hour and a half straight before my very first time on an airplane. After a panicky nudge from my mother, my dad took me aside, held my chin up with his forefinger and with a sigh told me not to worry. He found a long string that he would use to tie the airplane down to the ground with so that even in the sky, we'd be safe.

I sniffled a bit and rubbed my eyes. "I don't see it."

"It's an invisible string, Charlotte. I'll even let you keep it after the flight if you're a good girl and get on the plane for Mommy and Daddy. It'll keep you safe and out of trouble whenever you need it."

"Really?"

"Really, kiddo. Just trust me."

And I did.

Fast-forward ten years and he was stacking adoption agency pamphlets on my calculus book.

"Leave me alone," I groaned and pulled the covers over my head.

"Time to get up," he said as he slid the curtains open, welcoming in a strong ray of sunlight to blind my vision. It was noon on a Sunday and my parents were already irritated with me for sleeping through church.

"Dad, what are you doing?"

"You need to start looking through these options. They won't wait forever, you know." He waved a binder full of parent profiles from the adoption agencies at me. They wanted me to shop for your future parents in a catalog.

"There are some nice-looking ones. Look, here's a married Christian couple from Chicago. Newlyweds in Boston. A family with two other adopted kids already, and a dog."

I sat up in bed and stared at my father. The nausea was over with (thank God) but my hips felt unnaturally huge, my midriff heavy, and my sides cramped. I sighed and shook my head.

"Dad," I started. "I'm moving out."

He glanced up at me, dismissed my outburst as foolishness with a headshake, and looked back down at the catalog.

"With Keith, Dad. I'm moving in with Keith tonight and I've already made my decision—"

"You're getting married?" He blinked.

"What? No, Dad."

"Then, no," he said.

"Daddy, I'm not asking you for permission. I'm *telling* you."

"For God's sake, Charlotte, you're sixteen. You barely know how to boil water without burning yourself." He ran a hand through his hair and grimaced at me. "You were always such a good kid, I just don't understand."

"It's okay, Dad. He just got a new job and I'll be graduating soon and get one too. And I can work part-time for now and we'll take shifts."

"You were such a smart girl. Such a *good* girl. I should be teaching you how to drive, not lessons on parenting."

I looked down. Ran the corner of the pink leopard print cotton sheets through my fingers, looked back up.

He said, "I'm trying to help you as much as I can, Charlie." Pause. "We can look through these some other time."

Thinking of string.

The nurses were nice enough when I asked to stop before we even began. The doctor, all business, was out of there before I even had a chance to say something polite and inevitably strange, like *Thanks anyway! Thank you, but no thank you!*

It was still the first trimester then. I walked into the clinic that day, and I heard your heartbeat for ten seconds, and I just couldn't do it. Does that really make me a monster?

~

I suppose you're curious about Keith. He was sweet, at least in the beginning. During our first night living together he bought me yellow roses that I placed in a large plastic cup in the center of our dining room table and we cooked spaghetti for two with basil tomato sauce from a can. We finished half a pack of Oreos together for dessert and blew out the apple pie scented candles we lit for the evening and went to bed. I bought three different shades of green fabric and sewed throw pillows for the twin mattress we shared, frameless and bare.

We were just a couple of kids playing house. He'd go to work, a desk job at his school library, go to his classes at the community college in the afternoon, come home, eat dinner with me, make love to me, fall asleep, and start all over again. I still went to all of my classes too; Keith dropped me off at the high school on the way to work every morning. He wanted to transfer to a college in Southern California where his degree would be worth more and he'd make more money when he graduated. We talked of being a family, and I was dumb enough sometimes to dream up all the little details.

I dreamt that we'd go to all the ultrasounds and check-ups together. We'd move into an apartment with a spare bedroom, maybe even two, for guests and the future. Keith would build the crib himself and I'd paint it either pink or blue. We'd decide on a theme for the wallpaper and all of your sheets and toys, something like circus animals or *101 Dalmatians*, and that would be your little world. I'd turn my chin up as I passed brand baby food at the supermarket and make you homemade applesauce—I had no idea how, but I'd learn. And then I'd get creative, and add things like honey, cinnamon, and cranberry juice for an extra bit of taste, just to spoil you. I'd sew all your bibs myself, one to match each of your onesies, and we'd have all we'd ever need. We'd be simple and we'd be flawless.

Keith and I continued to finish our days together in bed and I'd curl up underneath one of his arms and try to hide my smiles. I'd hear things like *we'll make it through somehow* in Keith's voice, but he never really said stuff like that.

I'd call my parents every once in a while, but all they did was ask me where I was staying and what my plans were, and because I didn't want to answer, I stopped calling. Weeks passed and I started to show. We started to have less and less sex, cuddling got too hot and sticky, the bed got crowded. We would fight over the blanket with our eyes still closed.

Keith offered to take the couch. I said I would, and he seemed happy. I wanted, more than anything, for him to be happy.

A few nights into our new sleeping arrangement is when I started asking myself if something could be wrong between us. But I didn't like thinking about that before bed. I focused on furnishing our future home in Southern California, instead. They say Los Angeles is the city of dreams, but I always hoped we'd end up someplace like San Diego, some place just a little bit different.

We stopped lighting candles during dinner, and then stopped having dinner together at all. He'd come home late, sometimes kiss my forehead goodnight, sometimes not, and go to bed. I wanted, more than anything, for him to be happy.

I took the bus downtown to the mall and searched the maternity clothes section of every store that had one. Hours passed and I tried on every piece of sexy clothing I could find. Did you know they sell lingerie for pregnant women? I picked a pink silk slip with black lace trimming and matching panties.

I changed the minute I got home and waited for Keith to get back from class. I sat on the mattress. I crossed and uncrossed my legs about a dozen times. I leaned back and then sat up straight. I tossed my head around to make my hair look casually perfect.

He showed up at around eight o'clock and let out a little laugh when he saw me.

"What are you doing?" he asked.

"I missed you," I responded. "How was your day?"

"It was fine. I'm tired." He paused and pointed at the bed. "Am I allowed to go to sleep?"

"Not yet. Come sit down with me."

He did. I slipped my legs into his lap and tried to kiss him, but he flinched.

"What's wrong?"

"Charlotte. Just not tonight, okay?"

"Why not?"

"I don't know. I'm tired."

"You're always tired these days." I started rubbing his back. "You have so many knots. Just let me fix it, okay?"

"I don't want you to fix anything," he said.

"Why? You used to like my massages."

"I'm too tired," he said.

"But you don't have to do anything," I answered.

"Charlotte." Deep breath. "I'm going to bed, okay? I'm tired. Good night."

~

The truth is I hated feeling pregnant. I hated the stretch marks, I hated my tender breasts, I hated being perpetually hungry, and I hated the growing lump above my waist telling the whole world that you were there. I was bloated all of the time, you tugging at the inner boundaries of my skin until I felt like I was going to burst.

One morning when I was about six months along, my mom woke me up early by gently shaking my shoulder and telling me to get dressed. We were going to church, just the two of us.

It was never just the two of us. I'm not even sure how she got into my apartment. Keith, she told me later. She caught him right as he was leaving for work. She followed me a while ago and knew where we were staying for some time now. Had an impulse to come see me.

Our reverend-in-training led the study group that morning. Joshua, I believe his name was. There were nine of us total, including my mother and I. Shiphrah and Puah, two midwives from the book of Exodus, was our topic, Joshua announced.

"As we know from the book of Exodus, the Egyptians feared the growing Hebrew population…" started Joshua. I had trouble looking away from his nose hairs, which blew back and forth every time Joshua mumbled a hard vowel sound.

The rest of the story goes like this: Shiphrah and Puah were ordered by the Egyptian king to let any female baby delivered by a Hebrew mother live. If they were called to help with the birth of a male Hebrew baby, they were to make sure death was delivered to the child. The women refused, and agreed to tell the king when asked that all Hebrew women gave birth before the midwives arrived, and that is why they had to disobey the royal order.

Joshua asked us to think of a time when we, or someone in our community, was faced with a decision like Shiphrah and Puah. A time when we felt pressured by an authority or a group to do something different from our values.

It was a very Californian speech. How Reverend Joshua would have probably hated it if I pointed out the liberal nature of his inspirational question, how my dad would have reacted. Somehow, our little conservative community thrived in the most liberal place in the country. We weren't afraid to thrive.

My mother didn't seem to be paying much attention. She looked like she wants to whisper a secret to me.

"—I think we've all faced Shiphrah and Puah's battle. Peer pressure is everywhere we look these days. School, the workplace; you walk outside, and someone's trying to get you to sign something or listen to what they have to say; everywhere—"

"—Yes, I have to agree. Just the other day, my little girl started pounding her fists up and down in those little future shopper grocery carts they have now for kids to walk around with next to their parents. Anyways, she was throwing a fit because someone got it into her head that we should all be drinking coffee every day to stay awake. She's *five*–"

"—so many more kids are drinking at a younger age these days—"

"—One of our students at the youth center told us about the rape drug—"

"—Oh yes! So easy to get, it's terrifying—"

"—He was saying how shocked he was even the way people talk about each other these days, particularly these young men about women. I think he has a point there, what you say is so influential, so powerful—"

"—So true, such an important thing to be conscious of—"

This went on for twenty minutes or so.

Becky was there, good old Becky from school. She wasn't really listening either. I heard the woman next to her asking about where she was planning to go to college, and what she was going to study, and how wonderful all of her answers were. They were both loud whisperers.

Suddenly it all seemed so unfair. Girls like Becky going off to see the world. Girls like Becky doing whatever they wanted, and nothing happening to them. Nothing ever. I knew I was being a brat. That didn't make my urge to stand up and list every little terrible thing I knew Becky had ever done any less tempting—drinking, and lying, and sex, and anything else that would make these church aunties gasp and faint over sweet, sweet Becky—as if she was somehow responsible for everything that was happening to me. To us.

I decided that Life and Death, they must be twins. They must have split from the same beginning and multiplied across the earth to build an army fit to battle both one another and the shared foe of Fate. They must have trained out of their wits and bled the same wounds, but Death scratched his open and let it drain. Open wounds are susceptible, I know, but that also means they must bathe in the freshness of everything around them. And I suppose I could have avoided this, I could have saved us both, but aren't mistakes what it's all about?

Then the guilt arrived. The guilt always made me feel childish. A real privileged kid. *It's not fair. Please.* A ridiculous thought.

I knew it. I knew it all. But that didn't change the daydreams, the tears that surfaced when I wondered what was next. Clawing at my brain, angry at whatever reason I had for not imagining something wonderful like holding you in my arms, instead.

I've come to believe that I made a decision about you that day. About Keith, about me, about all of us. In my childhood church, out of all places.

Chapter Seven: Evie

The folder Hannah handed me at the doctor's office—the oh so dreaded folder—is snug beside me as I sit up in bed one Sunday afternoon, a place I hardly find myself in any day after seven a.m. My fingers linger upon the pale cover and slowly slide the front fold back an inch, so I can see the words:

Location: San Jose, Calif.
Type of Adoption: Closed
Date of custody shift: Novemb—

I slam the folder shut again.

Too real, too real, too real.

Closed adoption? Adoption?!

The familiar well of curiosity rises up inside of me once again. Only this time, it doesn't have anything to do with what you smell like, or what nickname you would have chosen for me if only you had raised me, or if we style our hair a similar way. Who is this secret family that wanted me, once, when I was destined to be flawless in the way only newborns can be?

A quick Google search makes for a good distraction, where I find a website called findmymother.com. I write the title of the site down on the notepad beside me and draw the baby bird from *Are You My Mother?* by Dr. Seuss in the margins. The funky double strands of hair at the top of his head keep me entertained for another minute or so. Then I start doodling the tired looking dog with the long ears the baby bird thought was his mother when he hatched, his real mother gone to get him food.

If this bird were a cuckoo, the story would have a very different ending. Cuckoos, who abandon their eggs in the random nests of other sorts of birds. When a baby cuckoo is born, always earlier than the other birds, she forces the other hatchlings out of the crowded nest and gathers an adoptive mother's love all for herself. This is how other birds are tricked by the cuckoo mother bird, tricked into raising a baby bird that isn't even theirs.

My sore neck carries my focus back and forth between my laptop screen and the folder on my lap for hours. This tab dance I'm doing online is useless. Random facts and aimless searches for something I'm not even sure is out there. Answers.

Braving the folder again, here is what I find: a tiny newspaper clipping falls out—a vertical one probably hidden right in the middle of a Sunday paper for the meticulous readers. Newborn me health records, which I've seen before, though never really inspected. The usual: five and a half pounds and sixteen inches. And then the unusual, the facts I haven't seen before: a closed adoption that never came to fruition. These were dated two full months after my birthday. There is no doctor's note, nor counselor's note.

The article is vague. It sounds like a rumor. A doctor no longer practicing still performing services on the side, illegally. Sometimes selling prescription drugs he shouldn't have access to, too. Caught and sent away. Something to do with a young woman and a baby, a procedure gone wrong.

Here is what else I learn online: it is called a salt saline abortion. Still effective during third trimester pregnancies, there is an injection of salt into the womb where a fully developed fetus inhales. It's an overdose of salt. Labor of the stillborn goes as usual a couple hours later. But I didn't die. I failed you, I didn't die.

I can't read this.

adoption

drowning

salt river

salt tears

heartbeats, heartbeats

dying

labor

early

                                  tiny

      salty, salty, the ocean is salty

                         living, dying, living

Why?

I wonder what a cuckoo mother would do if the chick she planted in another's nest found her twenty years later.

~

It all starts when Harold decided to pop a squat in the middle of arts and crafts.

Kind of. Okay let me back up.

There is a boy at the daycare named Will who is way too touchy. He is constantly rubbing my knees, trying to lace his fingers with mine, and shooting his little hand all the way up my shorts. I mean, the boob-grab is basically part of the job description when working with little kids, but come on now, at least buy me hot lunch first, buddy.

I think I've gotten a hang of this talking to children thing. The key is to keep your voice at a volume double to theirs at all times instead of trying to get each one of them to quiet down. Take a couple steps closer to them as you speak to make yourself look even taller than usual. This works nine out of ten times. With every child, aside from Will.

Is it embarrassing to admit that I have a soft spot for him—for Will? How it warms my heart when he fights the other kids to hold my hand when standing in line, or for a spot curled up in my lap during story time? Perhaps opposites do attract. I was never the troublemaker in the classroom. I liked to hide away at the corner desks, quietly doodling on the backs of multiplication worksheets or skipping around encyclopedia pages to find the descriptions that had pictures. I can't control Will. He's too sweet to squash with discipline.

As Alice sets up the little personal rugs the kids sit on and places a box of crayons next to each, I walk forward to where the kids are huddled— straight back, voice high—and ask someone to raise their hand and tell me a good rule to follow during quiet time. They all have their eyes on the extra art supplies and papers in the center of the circle. We try to do lowkey activities like this towards the end of the day so that when the parents start streaming in, they're not totally horrified.

After going through the *don't steal each other's crayons, don't bite each other* rule-setting portion of the day, the kids are finally settled and happy with their crafts. I look up pictures of different animated animals on my phone to outline on paper and let the kids color them in.

Then it all unravels. Five o'clock strikes: the baby apocalypse happens.

Daniel pulls Jessie's pigtails; Jessie starts shrieking; Harold takes off his pants and starts running around the circle, nude; Franco is in the corner eating crayons; I can't get Jessie to shut up; Will is clinging to my leg like a horny monkey; I can barely move; Harold stops running when he gets to the center of the room, pops a squat, and takes a crap.

At least it gets the room to quiet down.

Someone walks in to pick up a kid at this very moment, of course. Jessie smiles like she wasn't just bawling her eyes out a minute ago, hops up and gives the man a hug.

I usually love watching the kids get picked up. It's my favorite part of the day. And not because of the relief of getting them off of my hands. Forget the silly games, and annoying songs, and nonstop chatter about new movies I have never even heard of. When one of them gets picked up by a mom or a dad or a grandparent, the rest of them look like little adults. The way they all stop everything that they're doing and watch each other get picked up with distant, happy faces, just waiting for their turn. A little twinkle in their eye, a sad and happy hope. It's normally very cute.

There is nothing cute, anymore, about today.

I don't know why, but I start apologizing to this guy at forty miles an hour.

"No worries." He smiles and shakes his head. "Shit happens."

Ha. Ha.

"I know," I respond.

He says he's Jessie's father. He's cute. They have the same dark blue eyes and wavy brown hair.

I must be ogling, because as father and daughter walk out the building, I hear Alice laugh and say to me, "He's married."

I jump at her voice and pretend to retie my ponytail with the flimsy yellow hairband I need to throw away. The pair have now already trotted into the parking lot hand-in-hand.

"In case that matters," she adds.

"It doesn't." I blush.

I turn around and find the worst cleaning job of my life waiting for me.

Paper towel in hand, I allow myself to watch out of the corner of my eye as Jessie scoots into the minivan that has been waiting for her. Her dad removes the bag hanging from her right shoulder and places it in the trunk. When he settles into the passenger seat, a redheaded woman leans into the backseat and plants a kiss on Jessie's forehead. Jessie's father is saying something, and the redhead kisses his open lips as he finishes his sentence. I wonder what he is saying. Is it to her, to Jessie, to Jessie's older brother in the very back of the van, to Jessie's baby brother in the car seat, waving one of those fabric baby toys with plastic rings hanging off of it that looks so much like a chew toy? It's hard to tell.

Snap out of it. I do a little awkward dance as if I'm looking for a dropped contact lens somewhere around the window. Unconvincing, for sure. The last thing I need is to get caught teary-eyed, spying on strangers.

~

I am sitting, flexing my feet after walking along the Pacific, waiting for that moist-but-dry-sand-stuck-to-my-toes feeling to go away, when I realized something I haven't realized in a while. Maybe ever. I have absolutely no idea what I am doing. I have no plan. And it is terrifying.

I'm only a few blocks away from the bus stop, holding a pair of broken sunglasses and drinking tea from a café around the corner called *Mugs & Toes*, because tea is the cure for everything internal. Some people think that's true of alcohol, but they are wrong.

Here at the pier, the birds fly together, close to the sand, where earth and ocean meet. Their dips look like sideway carousels, every flick of a wing noted within the endless movement curving off of one another and it's so pleasant, and odd, and brilliant that I wonder why birds don't just stick to flying low, always. Who are they trying to impress? I think of how seagulls can survive drinking both fresh and salt water. I'm not sure if other animals can do this, belong everywhere at once, but seagulls sure can.

It turns out Hannah and Mitchell have been chatting about the folder some more, the visit to the doctor's office. Since when did she become such a Chatty Cathy? First the internship, now this. That woman never in hell shares any gossip with me.

This isn't new, Mitchell's ability to get so much more out of Hannah than I ever have. The truth about me and you gets Mitchell thinking. Inspired.

"I checked online," Mitchell says when he brings it up, yet again. He wets his lips and his eyes dart from side to side. We are in our snug kitchen, using cooking spray to fix a squeaky cabinet door. His speech grows loud and quick. "They have a volunteer committee for this sort of thing. Helping people find their parents, I mean. And with the notes from the folder, we could totally find her."

"Hello, genius, but those mean practically nothing. I don't know anything. I don't even have a birth certificate. Remember?" I shake the cooking spray bottle. I can't stand the fuzzing sound it makes when it begins to run out. So obnoxious.

I can tell Mitchell is noting how annoyed I'm getting. But telling him it's not because of him, but that stupid bottle, would just make me sound even more annoyed than I really am.

"What makes you think I *want* to find her anyways?" I continue. "I never said that. Why is this so important to you?"

"My parents are dead, Evie. You still have a chance to find yours."

I tell him I'll think about it.

To make my day even better, I woke up this morning with a tense leg cramp that needs icing. And I don't have my fucking pills. I haven't forgotten about my health insurance, which the state has so politely pulled the plug on.

During the next few days, I wait for a call from the disability medical insurance representatives and eventually get an estimate so high, I might as well forget about college, or rent, or anything of that money-spending nature. Translation: we don't actually want to pay your hospital bills. Thanks a lot.

After lying down in my listless state for half an hour, I place the icepack over my face and wonder if there's an icing time for reaching Zen.

It's at about this point of riding the self-pity train that I decide I need to jump off, quickly. Do something. Anything. I say I am going for a walk; I end up at the notorious pier instead.

Mindtrip away, I tell myself, as I swing my legs over the dock. *Fantasize, and dream, and all that crap. But just here.* Only here am I allowed to whisk myself away to the fantasyland I can't shake since you've stormed into my life. Only here can I wonder about what you were thinking, then. What are you thinking about right now?

I can scream for no reason at all other than pure frustration, I can cry, or I can just zone out and stop getting mad at myself for being distracted, for thinking of anything but the present. *Get it out now*, and when I step inside of my home again, I'll be better.

But that isn't really true. I imagine meeting you all of the time. Sometimes when it's quiet and I'm lying awake in bed, or maybe standing aimlessly in the shower, and my thoughts and I become acquainted, I let myself think of horrible, terrifying things. Things like you walking up the six colossal steps that lead to my doorway one wet October morning without an umbrella or a coat, asking for a place to dry off. And then leaving you standing in my empty hallway to get you the thickest towel I can find. Then, when I come back, the front door is shut, and you've disappeared.

Or walking through downtown one evening after work, the restaurants filled by twos, bars by threes or fours, it being Friday and gay and grand, and I see you sitting beneath yellow streams of hanging lights and a heat lamp, holding onto someone's arm—I can't see whose—laughs of thunder rolling off of your beige colored lips, and somehow just knowing that it's you and walking as usual past you without a word.

Every once in a while, I get fed up with these mindtrips, keep running around town with this itch that I can't scratch, go home and sit cross-legged beneath the showerhead while turning the water to its coldest. Hot, cold, hot, cold, hot. But I have a feeling that today this ritual will be of no use. I'm never getting you out of my head, am I? What would *you* do? I keep wondering as if it matters. You haven't found me, my childhood nights wrapped up in quilts and dreams and stillness, so I guess that's my answer.

The way the seagulls do it is they take in everything and let the glands right above their eyes flush the salt away. I sit with my legs dangling over the ocean water, and my sunglasses break in my restless hands, and the tea settles within me, and all I can think about is the washed-up ocean foam below me. How pathetically it shivers from the slightest gust of wind. That's what this would be, you and me, trying to work, after all these years. Why am I even considering looking for someone who so obviously doesn't want to be found?

True, I'd like to tell you a thing or two about my life. Not because you deserve it, or because I am naïve enough to think that you'd care. Only because sometimes silence can be a gift, and I wouldn't want to mistakenly bless you.

Most of all, I'd like to tell that family that they made a huge mistake, changing their mind like that. I can walk, I can talk, I can swim, what was everyone so afraid of? Then I look at my orphaned medical bills, and the obscure article about the doctor who went to jail, and I hate myself for thinking this, but can any of us really blame them?

Chapter Eight: Charlotte

The walls of the old church I grew up in always had a sort of tumbling feeling to them. They were not actually moving, of course, but there was something about the simple brown wallpaper on the inside. The plain wood on the out. The way sound bounced off the walls when we ran down the halls. The way the walls sweat a little bit during the summers. It was a visual warning, the same thing that every adult in between those walls always tried to tell us; today just might be the day everything that was built for us falls. Tumbling down. Like a mudslide that's been frozen in time.

The place hasn't changed much. Today I sit outside on the big concrete steps leading up to the double doors that make up the entrance and know just how much this is true. Here on the steps is where I'd play when I was too antsy to stay seated in the pews and my mother got tired of trying to tie me down. It felt like somewhere else, like Brooklyn, or maybe even Europe, or anywhere where sitting outside was a pastime.

I liked to snatch my mother's compact mirror from her purse during sermon when she wasn't looking and run away to the steps, see how far I could roll the compact down the handrail before it toppled over the side. When I'd get bored with that, I'd open the compact up and stare. I would try to see myself differently. A redhead, maybe. Or blue-eyed. I wanted to be quiet and beautiful, mysterious. To work a glamorous job as a magazine editor, overseeing a staff that needed me around desperately in order to get anything done. Or a flight attendant, living in a different city every night.

Why are these steps where I end up today, the first day that I am back in my hometown after such a long time? The place I haven't thought about in years, the place I tried to make feel like home for so long, and it just never did. It must be fate, it must be destiny, ending up at church today.

I roll my eyes at myself.

I wrote a letter to Destiny once. I told her how cruel she was. I told her how she must not know about the loneliness of the in-between. She must not know about being an almost. She must not know, she must not know.

The wind pushes my hair from one side to the other while leaving a cocktail of scents at my nostrils, heavy car fumes and moist, leafy sword ferns drifting down from the Santa Cruz Mountains. What a home I've come back to.

~

When I touch my mother for the first time in years, she feels like autumn. She crumbles in a way only living things know.

"Hi Mom." As I drag my lumpy, heavy suitcase in behind me, I've forgotten that I've missed her.

"Hi, beautiful. Welcome home." We're inside now, in the house we lived in together my entire childhood. For whatever reason, I'm surprised that age has made her look frail. But I know better. "I hope you're hungry," she says. "I made your favorite."

"Yeah, thanks," I say. "You look different."

"You look the same," she answers. Then she laughs. She pushes my hands away when I try to stop her from carrying my luggage to the guestroom, a bare version of my bedroom growing up. The place looks washed away somehow. Pale. Even the bedsheets I know must be new look worn out—I've never seen them before.

"So, how have you been?" I ask. That was dumb, wasn't it? Could I be any more formal with this woman?

She looks surprised. "Fine. Great. Though it's been so quiet around the house ever since your father passed. No one to bicker with." She laughs again. "But it is great to have you home. Finally."

She smiles a sad and lovely smile and leads me to the kitchen. The tea kettle hums and the dying gas stove whistles a low goodbye as my mother scoops some gingered yam soup into two blue ceramic bowls. The green and yellow floral print paper napkins serving as centerpieces in the metal napkin holder are folded in half as they always are, the circular wooden dining room table is chipped in all the same places—no more, no less. The woman is the same, but with pale hair brushed back into a low ponytail instead of being done up in a proper bun like it used to always be, and she's wearing a flannel shirt and black yoga pants instead of one of her pleated dresses. This girl who grew up here so long ago is a woman now, too, with broader hips and smaller dreams, the stale scent of familiarity still lingering in the air.

We sip our soup quietly. My mother is the only woman who still uses the fireplace religiously on the West Coast, and the air becomes toasty and easy to lean back into. Above the mantelpiece are five photos framed in matching yellow frames. My school photos: age five, in a sweater with an image of a kitten on it knit by my mother, and age eleven, in braces and frizz that didn't make it all the way into the shot. A Christmas postcard of the three of us wearing matching red cardigans in the backyard (Dad planted grapes that year, if for nothing but some aesthetic vine photos). The other, a much earlier photo, in Disneyland. The center photo is larger than the rest, one of my parents linking arms beneath a rosewood tree on their wedding day.

I know the dull comfort will simmer away soon. Coming back to your childhood home is like that, a vicious black hole with all your favorite things in it. It sucks you away from reality and slams your face right smack in the middle of it at the same time.

I know she wants to talk about him. I know she knows he is the real reason that I left. But I'm not ready.

"I'm not sure if you have any other plans for the day," Mom starts as she tips her bowl and swirls her spoon around to get the last of her soup. "Heck, you just got here. I have a couple errands to run. Do you want to join? See the town? Make my life a little easier and pick out what you want to eat for the next couple of days. I don't even know what sort of food to buy for you anymore."

"Huh? Oh, I eat everything," I say. "I think I'll pass on shopping this time."

"How about a walk around the neighborhood, then?" she asks after a brief pause. "I bet you're just itching for some fresh air after being locked up in an airplane for so long."

"No, thanks," I say as I start to clear the table. "Thank you, though. Let's do something together tomorrow, okay? I'll help you pack up the house."

She asks again about grocery shopping as I place the washed dishes on the drying rack. And then, she asks again.

"I said no." I can hear how I sound. But I just can't help it. Mothers always bring the teenagers out of us, even when we're all grown up, don't they?

I was prepared for an awkward arrival, not seeing my mother for so long. I was even prepared for the confusing mess of emotions, the I-missed-this-place-but-not-really. What I was not prepared for was the strong desire to do anything, *anything* but step foot outside of this house. Suddenly running into everyone and everything that stayed behind doesn't just sound unpleasant, it sounds like the most terrifying, and inevitable, thing in the world. What is the harm in putting it off a little longer? What does one say when "figuring it out" isn't an exciting answer anymore?

Mother gives me a weird look after I snap at her, and finally grabs her reusable grocery bags and car keys before heading out the door, alone.

I didn't just come here because my mother asked me to. I came here because after years and years of dragging around time with me like an old keepsake, I've finally unclenched my fists to find nothing. It has slipped away. Or maybe it was never there to begin with, at all. All I know, now, as I near my forties is that my decades-old escape plan doesn't do it anymore. It's expired. I must remap. The best way to start is from the beginning.

~

I never thought I could hear silence. Not until Keith gave up. During the day he disappeared and during the night he came home smelling of perfume and cheap liquor, only to lock the bedroom door behind him, lock me out with widened eyes, a steady pressure beneath my forehead, the sudden roar of stillness ringing in my eardrums, and there I'd be pressing pillows tightly over my ears to stop the sound of silence. I hated silence.

The couch was too narrow for me to spread my swollen ankles out comfortably and the stiffness of the armrest agitated my back to the point where I preferred the floor. I'd curl up in a fetal position on the rug, wait till drowsiness overtook my eyelids, and dream up a different life for us in San Diego.

I woke up face down on the carpet to the smell of sour milk and a strong scent of meat that made me want to hurl. I forced myself up onto my feet and saw Keith sitting at the kitchen table watching me. My belly bulged in its last trimester, but I kept forgetting you were actually real.

"Morning, baby," I mumbled and kissed his cheek. He flinched faintly, but I noticed. I pretended not to.

"How'd you sleep?" he asked.

"Fine."

"I'm working another double shift tonight." He got up and started for the door. "Just so you know."

"Don't forget about our doctor's appointment at noon, though."

"I can't go," he said.

"It's one of our last checkups," I whined.

"Can't."

"Keith, this is important. I need you to be there."

"You've gone to doctor appointments before on your own. You're a big girl."

"Yeah, but don't you want to come? It's like you don't even care about our family."

He laughed.

"That wasn't supposed to be funny."

"I'm paying for this, aren't I?"

"That's not what I meant." Silence. "I can't even drive, Keith, how am I supposed to get there?"

"Call your dad."

"Very funny."

He turned toward me. "I'm serious. Call your dad and have him pick you up. I'm tired of this. I can't be doing this."

"Doing what?"

"Look, Charlotte, you don't have to, either. It's not too late. I know this guy that can help you—"

"Help *us*."

My arm burned from the rug, a reminder of Keith coming home late last night. My head snapped up as he talked and talked, and for the second time that year, I grabbed my bag, stuffed the few belongings I had in it without a word, and walked out the door.

It hit me that I was pregnant, that I was really *really* pregnant; there was a baby growing inside of me. I was scared. I was young. I wasn't ready. I know excuses are nothing but clichés.

~

I have always loved a good story. My mother, who had me later in life than most and wasn't one for crawling, or running, or much besides sitting, would tell me a new story every day after I came home from elementary school. We liked hearing stories from different parts of the world. She'd have a snack laid out for me, ask about my day briefly, and would begin.

We agreed that the best story we ever read together was about Princess Savitri, who chased after the God of Death as he carried away her husband's soul. The god admired her devotion and said he would grant her three wishes—anything, except the life of her husband. She wished to restore her father's kingdom and eyesight, for her father to have many more children, and finally, to mother many of her husband's children. Being a man of his word, the God of Death had no choice but to release Savitri's husband to grant her final wish.

For what it's worth, I always thought that I was chasing the God of Death. For him, for you, for us. Like clever Savitri. I'm sorry about how wrong I was.

Chapter Nine: Evie

Tiptoeing around Mitchell is incredibly tiring. For one thing, he has the sneaky footing of a cat. Just when I think I can feel the heaviness of sleep seeping from the bottom crack of his closed bedroom door, take the cue from the lonesome hallway to hurry across the way to the kitchen in my fuzzy house slippers with the padded bottoms for an extra hush, and start the most amazing breakfast-making experience of my life after hiding behind my own bedroom door for twenty-five minutes with a pissed off stomach, he gets me.

At first, I'm quiet about it. Slowly sliding out our shared skillet from the bottom drawer of dishes and whatnots. The perfectly square block of butter I cut off melts from the outside in, like petals being pulled back and away from the pistil. Letting minutes pass and the focused state of my eyes pass with it. Two egg yolks spread after the butter's route. Then I sprinkle a handful of sliced tomatoes in, sweet onions that are thinly sliced, a bit of salt, green bell peppers, orange bell peppers just to make it pretty—

"Morning, sunshine," he says from behind me. I nearly hit myself in the face with the spatula. He waves his keys in front of me to show me that he was up early, just got back. He places two brown paper bags full of groceries on the counter.

I owe Mitchell an answer. I know, I know. I shouldn't hide from him, it's immature. But I just can't seem to find a response. I've sat in showers long enough, arm wrestling with the shower handle from cold to hot, cold to hot, and still haven't come up with anything. Isn't that the place where answers find people? Showers?

He's looking for an adventure, and he's found one in our story. It's why he looked for those parent-finding sites. I know he'll say it was for me, at the end of the day, but I know this is only part of the truth. He's an adventure seeker. Adventure seekers hardly ever sit still. I can see the itch he's asking to scratch.

I turn the stove off, the flipside of the omelet probably too crisp to be any good at this point, and pull my red Toms on. I think of going for a walk. Mitchell unpacks cans of black beans and chicken noodle soup from one of the grocery bags and looks at me expectantly.

"There's nothing I can do," I finally say.

"Aren't you at least a little bit curious of what she has to say?"

"If she had something to say, she would have said it by now," I challenge.

Mitchell gives me a look.

"Fine," I grumble and get up on my feet. My car keys sing as I swing my purse onto my shoulder, Mitchell's dimpled smile following me to the driveway.

~

When we knock on Hannah's door, unannounced, she greets us with a confused look and stares for a few seconds before asking us to come in, as if this is the first time she's ever seen us in her life. I am not the least bit surprised. She sits us down at the kitchen table and pulls out her weekly organizer booklet to find out if the little box that says 1:00 p.m. today is filled out yet or not. She does this whenever Mitchell or I ask her if she would let us take her out for lunch on her birthday or would like to go on a walk on a weekend morning, making sure she hasn't forgotten any plans. Us being unexpected visitors, and all. We wait for her to give the OK before we start talking. I could have walked through this entire visit with my eyes closed and not missed a bit. Hannah is so predictable.

Some people just call it being organized. Type A. Not the emotional type. Have you ever suddenly doubted a first impression of someone you've known for years? Perhaps my feelings towards Hannah were always based off of Mitchell's. Mitchell and Hannah laugh together more than she and I do.

After setting her organizer back on the bookshelf nearby, Hannah fills my chipped "I Love Monterey" mug with black coffee. The pot sizzles slowly as

Hannah places it back on its damp hot plate, and the hummingbird-shaped kitchen timer besides it goes off with rhythmic chirps, announcing that the potatoes in the oven are ready.

"Are you hungry?" Hannah asks as she folds up the cardboard box the potatoes came in and places it in the plastic garbage can she uses for recycling.

"No, thanks," I reply.

"What can I do for you?" she asks after sitting back down across from us, her fork grazing the white insides of a potato slice.

"How are you?" I ask.

"Fine," says Hannah. She carves her fork into the potato's flesh and takes a bite from the crispy edge.

I blink at her a couple times.

"You know, Hannah and I found these the other day," says Mitchell from where he's wandered off to. He clears his throat and begins pushing around a few papers on the coffee table, looking for something. I pretend the fact that he's casually been hanging around Hannah's house doesn't sting. Meanwhile, Hannah and I haven't talked in sixteen days and six hours. Until today. But hey, who's counting?

Mitchell holds up a pair of plastic Little Mermaid sunglasses. "Remember these?"

"My glasses." I accept and turn the cereal box goodie around in my hand, it being about the size of my palm.

"I couldn't get them off of you," Hannah says.

"You were obsessed," Mitchell calls from the living room, where he hops back onto the couch and swings his feet onto the coffee table.

"A and B conversation, dork," I say back. "And no, I wasn't."

"You made us call you Eel-ie," he says.

Mitch and Hannah laugh.

I really did. After watching *The Thirteenth Year* on Disney Channel, I had this dream that the mute mermaid mother was actually mine. So, obviously, I was part fish. I still wasn't allowed near the water, then, so Hannah and Mitchell taught me how to swim on our living room carpet.

That August night when I stopped wearing the sunglasses, Hannah's Basque shepherd got run over by a truck. Hannah offered to take me, Mitchell, and the two extras of the month to the shelter to pick out a new puppy, but we didn't want to. We never wanted another dog again. It seemed wrong.

Mitch didn't talk much for the next two weeks, then slowly lost interest in mourning. I became fascinated. I read books on different afterlife theories and healthy living magazines. I started taking myself out on daily walks around the block. I started saving up for a gym membership, even though I was too young for one and was terrified of all the exercise equipment, anyway. I stretched three times a day even when it hurt. Something about shaking hands with mortality for the first time made me want to throw away the glasses and drive myself for miles along the edge of reinvention.

Hannah told me it was okay to be sad sometimes, but that it was important to "keep going." The seasons changed and I ran like hell through the stillness only winter brings, just to try and figure out what in the world "keeping going" even means.

~

"I wanted to ask you," I start, pulling out my notepad where I've jotted down the few hints I have leading to you. I think I can see Hannah's vision sharpen. Her assignment, her purpose. "Do you know what hospital I was born in? Or anything about where I came from?"

"No," she responds. She waits politely with her hands folded in front of her.

"So, there's nothing you can share with me?"

"No." Hannah shrugs. "No one ever knew much about you. Or your biological family."

We're still sitting at her kitchen table. After she finishes up her meal, we watch as Hannah wipes down the counter for crumbs with a damp towel and points to some old flowerpots in the corner of the kitchen. She was going to move them out back but it hurts to bend over. A pulled muscle in her back, she thinks. Mitchell volunteers us for the job.

"But Hannah," I say, giving Mitchell a *can we focus, please?* look. "The papers you gave me have tons of information. It says there was an abortion attempt." There is a stale silence for a bit. Not too sad, not awkward, just silent. "I never knew that," I add quietly.

Hannah shrugs, as if to say, *maybe there was, maybe there wasn't. I was not there to call it.*

You know how some people say they are all ears? I've known Hannah my whole life and I've never thought all ears was inherently a good thing. Hannah is all ears most of the time. Impressionable as an empty canvas, matter-of-fact as an open book. She tells it how it is and is surprised by overly animated reactions. She is caring by nature, consistently there for others only because she doesn't realize there is any other way. I've wondered for so long if that is what genuine kindness looks like, or if it's all the other way around—if the kindest acts are from those who are capable of the absolute worst.

I sigh. "Do you know anything else? Any names of foster care workers who can help us get more information, maybe?"

"Of course I don't know anything else." She looks surprised by the question. "How could I?"

After Hannah does her nervous little song and dance, I finally give in. "I guess you couldn't," I say.

~

"We better start taking Thornbush Street to Hannah's house," says Mitchell. "The highway is getting so ridiculous around here."

"*Hannah's* house, *Hannah's* house—why is it we always talk about that place as 'Hannah's house'?" Right away I know this has come out totally wrong. I really meant for it to be something ironic for us to roll our eyes at together and maybe even laugh about a bit. But it ends up sounding sort of angry. I blush.

Mitchell raises an eyebrow. He's driving us back to the apartment after our visit. He stops the thumb tapping against the steering wheel thing he always does when he's driving. He must be listening to some invisible soundtrack in his head whenever he's on the road. "What do you mean?" he asks.

"We both lived there for most of our lives," I say.

Back to thumb tapping.

~

"You're approaching her as if she's confrontational. As if she were you," says Mitchell.

"What's so horrible about that?" I ask.

"Nothing horrible. Just not her style."

We keep moving Hannah's flower vases back and forth between our small balcony and the bit of counter space we have left in the kitchen. *Not the right lighting*, Hannah finally concluded when we tried a few different spots for the pots around her home. She suggested we just take them with us.

"You keep wanting her to talk about her feelings, but she doesn't do that. It's hard for her," Mitchell says. "She can't just say what she wants."

"How the hell do you know what she wants? She's like a wall. No emotions. Ever."

"Evie, don't be stupid. You know her just as well as I do."

Maybe you think my relationship with Hannah is a weird one. Most people would. An old high school buddy Mitchell and I befriended to help us sneak into movies sometimes at the theater he worked at once defined it as "the booty call of parenthood."

Essentially, here is what we deem an acceptable communication cycle:

1. Remind ourselves that at the age of eighteen, I became an independent adult. I am an adult. I am such an adult. I make any medical decisions about my body all by myself without agencies now, I could go anywhere I want and do anything I please without permission—assuming I have the financial means—I can vote, I can gamble, I pay for everything. Living quarters, food, clothes, the whole deal. I am an adult. I am such an adult.

2. Ask Hannah for help with something. She says yes. I am an adult. I am such an adult.

3. Hannah executes without fail. What a hard worker she is.

4. Evie, that's me, pretends not to get sentimental about some sweet memory—the movie about mice singing Christmas carols none of us can ever remember the name of but we would watch every year just the same, little Evie yelling at Hannah for pulling at her hair too hard when she used to brush it, *the Little Mermaid* sunglasses. When Evie gets sentimental, Hannah drifts.

The drift is slow. She talks less, though she is never much of a talker anyway. She nods a bunch, in a way that reminds me of how some people nervously blink too much. She starts talking like a monotone corporate phone recording. She drops in the word eighteen as much as she can.

Social workers have different theories. Distance and control, they are similar sometimes. I saw quite a few social workers facilitate biological family relationships, "in a controlled environment," they would say. Most foster kids go back to their biological families at the end of things, because where else is there to go when you become an adult overnight? *Better to have a controlled environment than a disaster*, they say. I don't know. I certainly wouldn't wish for a disaster. Control is a complicated thing any way you spin it.

I was always fascinated with social workers. If it weren't for marine biology, maybe I would want to become one. Weird—you would think I'd hate them or something, right? Get as far away from the system as I can? Maybe it's the closeness, the student wanting to be the teacher, the usher to the actor, the bookworm to the author. But the social workers stayed away from me for the most part. I was set in the system and Hannah was mine. I think they probably thought I was too intense of a child, not the cute smiles of the little ones or the challenging angst of the teenagers.

I've thought of telling Hannah not to speak to me anymore multiple times. *There is no need*, I would say, *do not feel obligated. Eighteen has passed.* But

I don't say it. It's hard to. How do people just exit each other's lives without making a scene? People, like everything else, need to be balanced, taken in moderation. She would laugh so lightly I can almost see her wave me away with her voice. *Too intense* everyone always says of me.

Chapter Ten: Charlotte

The old house begins to breathe again at eight o'clock sharp on a Friday night. When I walked in earlier, it only exhaled.

Bayside Street is cluttered with cars, bumper to bumper. Friends I didn't know my mother had scurry in packs. She's really gone all out tonight, with a few random guests walking around holding platters of five different sorts of cheeses and three different sorts of saltless crackers to choose from, champagne fuzzing at the brim of dozens of stemless flutes, a guitar strum coupled with Portuguese lyrics in the background. She is parading across the party in a long black dress with nude laced sleeves. Nude laced sleeves! This home has never seen anything so over the top, I'm sure of it.

When the guitar playlist dies down, someone starts playing Billy Joel's *Vienna* on the piano. *Clever*, I think.

These goodbyes are meant to expire after six months, but who knows. Maybe she'll find herself an Austrian lover and stay there forever. She's recently read *Eat, Pray, Love* and I think she took the whole ticket to find yourself thing too literally.

"I'm excited to find myself, really find myself," she keeps saying. "And yes. I tried just looking in the mirror. Wasn't enough." She laughs every time. She goes on about how silly it is to claim contentment with ourselves without fully understanding who we are, what we are capable of, what we are made of. And, where we come from. So off to the land of our ancestors she goes.

I look for refuge in the kitchen with the extra spinach dip—the only people who walk back here are my mother and Mrs. Garrett from next door, who doesn't seem to recognize me, anyhow. The pigs in a blanket will be ready soon.

"Mom," I start as someone loosens a belt and straddles a bottle of champagne between the legs, fighting the cork with the edge of a steak knife. "Who are these people?"

But my mother isn't listening. She is hushing the stereo and pulling out my old Twister board. Twister. The woman is in her early seventies, for God's sake. Now I know why I hardly recognize any of these people. If any of our old church friends saw this, well, wouldn't Mrs. Anderson finally completely losing it after her husband's death just be the greatest Sunday morning gossip? The spinning arrow that tells you which body part to move to which color is shoved into my hands.

Right foot on red. Right hand on blue. Left hand on yellow. Someone places his hand on a spot beneath my mother's stomach and that gets her giggling for a good sixty seconds. Okay, next! Hurry, damn it. *Right hand on yellow. Left foot on green.*

A woman wearing a dark blue suit and a man in a matching tie put the music back on and start a little salsa number. Applause follows. But my mother still wants to play. *Left hand on blue.* They stare at me blankly. I yell the command over the music some more, turn to ask the dancers to turn the music down, and then let my eyes linger for a second longer by the door. A man with dark scruff and light eyes lets himself in, and he's not too bad to look at. He must be a bit older than I am, but not by much. Not exactly one for this crowd.

Left hand on blue. Right foot on yellow. He takes a couple slow steps towards the kitchen, stops, scratches his eyebrow with the inside of his thumb, and walks back out the front door. Then I drop the spinner, because I realize I finally found someone I know around here. And I don't like it.

I don't see her, but my mother is eyeing me, I know it.

"Ben," I whisper to the house. No one can hear me. I go after him.

Suddenly, I am on the sidewalk outside of my childhood home with Ben. Somehow, he's here, waiting for me. "Ben. Hi."

"Hi," he replies. He points to my mother's red minivan, which one of my mother's new friends just pulled into the driveway and turned off. The man picks up a few packs of beer from the backseat and eyes us as he carries them inside. "Your taillights are out," Ben says.

"What? Oh! Well, thank goodness you're here to tell us. Don't know what we would have done. I'm sorry, that sounded...I just didn't know you were coming tonight, is what I mean."

"I didn't either." He shrugs. "I got an invitation in the mail a while ago. From your mother, I'm guessing. Thought it was pretty random. How have you been? What have you been up to?"

You have some explaining to do, missy, the creases in his forehead seem to be saying to me, loud and clear above his raised eyebrows.

"Oh you know." I gesture at the house behind me. "Same old. Want to sit?" I wave at one of the steps leading up to the front door.

And then he tells me everything. All those life updates people swap. He was married for seven and a half years, divorced for two. He has a three-year-old son, who loves *Star Wars* and sour candy. He lives alone on weeknights, and with his son every other weekend. He still works at the firm—he's senior partner now.

Benjamin Wagner was always the perfect lawyer. He worked his way up from carrying mugs full of strong coffee for the executives to the position everyone assumed would just be handed to him from the start, it being his dad's company and all.

Most of the people we worked with together have switched out by now, gone on to the same job at a different place, or given the law up for something else entirely. He goes to the gym around the corner from my childhood home. He's seen my mother at a few charity events over the past few years and runs into her at the farmer's market every once in a while. He still sniffs his yogurt before he eats it. He still hates mornings, and tries to avoid early meetings now that he has more flexibility at the firm and he has become somewhat of a night owl because of it. He looks the same, with thinner hair that sticks up at the sides instead of carefully slicked back like it used to be.

"I wanted to talk to you so many times," tries Ben. "About what happened. What really happened. But I had no idea where you even disappeared to." He ends with a hoarse, short laugh.

~

Ben thinks I'm dishonest. He did then, and he still thinks so now, I can tell. It isn't true. Not really.

High school was something to just get through, as far as I was concerned, especially after I gave you up. I needed out, and I needed it fast. I took summer classes and doubled up on English and math credits to graduate a semester early. I wasn't sure what my plan was anymore. It kept changing. Law school, admin work at my dad's office, volunteer work overseas, anything. Something else. No option sounded right. I wanted to spread a picnic blanket out in front of the Eiffel Tower with some grapes, a good French magazine I didn't understand with a glossy cover featuring a pretty French girl, and one of those personal-sized French baguettes. I wanted to ride a gondola in Venice and be sung to, or get a waitressing job in London and pretend to have a British accent. I suppose that means I was naïve, or ignorant, or some other word people always use to describe their younger selves. I suppose I wanted to find myself.

What I actually ended up doing after graduating from high school: signing up for a couple classes at community college while living in my childhood bedroom and continued signing up for classes until I got my associate's degree in paralegal studies.

My first day at Wagner & Associates was a miracle day. It snowed in the Bay Area.

Well, not exactly, because it only lasted for five minutes and melted quickly instead of fluffing at the ground. After the hysteria, people figured out it was actually sleet, not snow. But trust me; I knew it was snowing before I even got out of bed that morning.

Walking to work really did feel like being in one of those snow globes, magic and all. I felt on top of the world in my first-ever business suit and my mother's old leather purse instead of my jean shoulder strap bookbag. Life was different now and I understood what it meant to be here, walking in this snow globe of a world. It could all get shaken up again at any time.

I decided right there and then that if anything out there was going to change things, shake things up, make me start over—that thing better be me.

~

About three weeks passed since my first day at Wagner & Associates and I'd finally gotten a hang of the whole call forward thing, the endless blinking of voice messages piling up, the routine of filing papers that made me a young professional now.

I still didn't have very many friends. I thought being in a new place, a fresh start, meant a new me. But I felt the same as I did in high school.

Then Ben found me one day three minutes before the all-firm meeting we had every Friday. I was walking back to my desk from the restroom and he stopped me with a smile and an introduction. We shook hands. Attorneys weren't making small talk with paralegals very often in this office, and he wasn't even my direct supervisor.

"You're the new paralegal, right?"

I nodded.

"Welcome to Wagner & Associates," he said. "How do you like it so far?"

"It's great," I told him. "Everyone's really nice."

"I hope Randy isn't bombarding you with too much work just yet," he said with a smile. "He's a tough one."

"No, he's been really helpful. He's taught me a lot already."

"Good, good." He winked at me. "Your enthusiasm is blinding, you know, for someone who's having such a great time here."

"What?"

"Sorry. Just teasing. I do that."

"Oh." I tried to laugh, but it came out sounding so awkward, he responded with a "bless you."

"It is tough being new here, huh? I remember," he said.

"I guess it'd be nice to have a social aspect," I responded. "I didn't really get much of that in community college and with living at home and all."

He nodded and we chatted a bit more about the all-staff meeting.

"You know, a bunch of us sneak out for drinks after Friday meetings sometimes if you want to come," he said.

I said I did. Never mind that I was underaged.

~

"Is this a *date*?"

"Only if you want it to be," Ben said.

I watched Tamara, another paralegal, and Randy, my supervisor, slobber all over each other about a foot away from me. We—Tamara, Randy, Ben, and I—were sharing a booth at the bar. I was shocked to find out adults still do that sort of thing in public.

Ben drank his tall rum and coke straight out of the glass instead of through the thin, black mixing straw the way everyone I knew did. I didn't order anything, not even food, so they wouldn't think to card me. That left me with nothing to do but stare at Ben. His hair was starting to thin, and I noticed the little wrinkles beginning to form at the corners of his eyes. I found it really sexy. He was successful, and a leader, and gentle. And I liked that. I suddenly became very aware of myself, wedged between horny lawyers and a beautiful, terrifying man. I wished I had at least asked for a glass of water earlier when the waiter came by. It'd be something to do with my hands.

"I can drive you home if you want to leave," Ben whispered to me so that the others wouldn't hear.

When I just blinked at him, he added, "you don't seem like you want to be here. It's okay."

"No, it's not that," I said. "I just—I've gotten out of a very bad relationship. And ordinary things like going out with coworkers just seem so strange now. Everything does. But also refreshing at the same time. And I don't want to mess up."

"Ah. A girl with a past."

I nodded.

"You know what that means, don't you?"

"That I'm screwed up for life?"

"No," he said. "That you call the shots from now on, kid. It's all you."

I smiled.

"You…you are kind of like that hand," he said as he pointed at the side table to his left. It was a single wooden leg twisted upwards, like a vine, holding up a flat glass top. Intricately carved wooden hands attached all around the vine-like table leg, the fingers curving around, clutching in a desperate manner. Truthfully, it looked kind of tacky. And that corny line. He was definitely beginning to feel his drink. "It's strong, and all. You can tell by the way it's shaped. Instead of moving up the vine like the rest, it's fallen behind. You'll get back up there. It'll feel strange at first like you said, things like this, meeting new people, but you'll get back up there."

I wanted to laugh, but he finally turned his head back towards me and without a single slur in his words, he said, "no pressure, Charlotte. I'll be here when you need me."

We ate pretzels from the bar until he sobered up. He drove me home and I leaned over to give him a hug when he pulled over outside of the house. He seemed surprised. I pulled back half an inch and brushed my lips softly against his and kissed him.

And so began my adventures with the criminal attorney, Ben Wagner. I didn't give up on falling in love, I suppose. I was still a little disappointed when it didn't happen right away. Instead we talked some days after work or at lunch, like friends. I was touched to be asked things nobody every bothered to ask me—what I thought about the upcoming elections, what I thought about religion, if I'd raise my kids the way my parents raised me.

"We're so grown up," I remember saying with a sway during another night out once the alcohol I'd been quietly sipping earlier began pulling me in for a warm hug from within. I was bolder during these happy hours now, and got in the habit of stealing Ben's glass.

He politely didn't say anything, let the comment slip. He didn't get what I meant. I was looking at him, Ben, but I must have been speaking to Keith. My mother once told me that I always see the best in people, and that would be my own downfall.

~

I think about that a lot right now, my own downfall. It's seated beside me, cocking an eyebrow at me. Asking me where I've been. Here, on the steps of the home that raised me, minutes from the farewell party my mother threw for herself.

At one point, I convince Ben to go inside to get some food without me. Just to stop *that look*, the expectant one.

Ben will always be the lovely, quiet man that loves a good argument, the one that never taps his foot while waiting in long lines or gives the gas pedal too strong of a nudge that moment rush hour traffic finally frees up. I will always be the silly girl with a big life who couldn't speak when he whispered words like *love* to me.

Chapter Eleven: Evie

I never thought the day would come, but Alice is stern. Jessie pouts her lip and stomps her feet; she refuses to put her floaties on in the pool. She's the only one of the kids who doesn't know how to swim yet.

"Uncomfortable in water," her mother said from the front seat of her car last week when we first announced daily swim lessons in the afternoons for the older kids, four- and five-year-olds. "All of them. On land, I can't get them to sit down for one minute. But in water." She held up both arms and tensed into a 'freeze' position. "They just clam up."

Jessie's brothers were watching the Scooby Doo Halloween Special from the backseat. I think I remember that one. Scooby Doo dresses up as a ghost and then disappears.

"Sometimes it helps to swim with them, I think," I said, but she was already turned to the backseat, shaking her head as her oldest son tried to wiggle a third fruit roll-up out from her purse.

As Jessie's fit continues, so does Alice's frustration. The woman, believe it or not, becomes a believer in the tablet babysitter. Enough to keep Jessie entertained while the rest of the kids swam.

The whole reason this swim thing became a thing was to get a leg up on the other daycares in the neighborhood. The Center now guarantees at least two swim days a week as part of the regular daycare program. We cannot make other plans on Tuesday and Thursday afternoons. It is important that we swim, management told us.

I'm delighted to see Alice act human. Up until today, I was constantly wondering if she was just plain imaginary.

It's not just her endless positivity. Or the weird, highly inappropriate moments she instigates. She stares openly at people. She doesn't have much of a filter. She says things like "potty" and "ouchy" when there is not a child in sight, it's just the way she speaks.

An example. One day she asked me, in front of all the kids, if I was happy.

"You're blushing," she noted with a smile.

"It's a silly question," I responded.

We were standing on opposite sides of the rooms, with a sea of children seated between us. It was story time, and she was waiting for me to dig through our limited pile of books until I found one that we have not read to this group of kids yet. I couldn't stop thinking about that moment all day.

Another example. Today, all the kids are already rinsed off after the swim of the day and dressed. Alice is folding up unused towels and I'm scraping off an enormous blob of bubble gum from my flip-flops as a teenage counselor-in-training walks the troops back in for an art project. I'm already frustrated because Jessie threw a fit when I tried to take the tablet away from her, once the rest of the kids were out of the water and ready to go. She wasn't finished with the video she was watching.

Foolishly, I thought we'd bond over the fact that we are both having such a hard time today, Alice and I. A *tough day, huh?* kind of moment normal colleagues might have.

"I'm thinking maybe I'm going to fire you," Alice says instead out of the blue.

"What?"

"I think you'll thank me one day," Alice continues.

"Are you out of your mind?"

"No, I'm not. I think it's a good idea because…" Her voice trails for so long, I think she has forgotten what she is talking about. "There might be something else you're really good at," Alice concludes.

I stare at her in a way I know recharges me. Courage fills me up to the brim. *I've had it up to here*, I want to say to her, the way I almost did with Jessie and that stupid tablet. The words have been dancing on the tip of my tongue for a long time now.

"I'm coming back here tomorrow," I answer, turning my back, rolling my eyes. "I don't want to, but I will. I won't do that to the kids. You need my help around here, anyhow."

She puts her arms up in surrender. "Okay, okay, Evie. Come by during swim time tomorrow." Alice wipes her feet, paddles back into a room full of children eager to hear her read from a storybook in the funny voices that she does sometimes. "Teach Jessie how to swim," she says when she looks back at me one last time. Then she sits on the crowded rug and immerses herself completely into the untroubled world of smiles and children.

~

Nothing happens the next day at work for me to be bothered, really. Everyone behaves. Alice is pleasant to a respectable degree. There isn't a lot of traffic and I'm feeling well, healthy.

No one is ever proud of their outbursts. The whole *I'm fine but not really* act. I shouldn't blame everything on this sweet, kind woman who hired me when no one else would. I should know Mitchell recommended this stranger to me for a reason.

I was thinking about a mother who walked in that morning. I've never seen her before. I don't know all the parents. Pick-up small talk isn't my favorite thing. Usually a trainee steps in for those necessary smiles and comments about the weather, and I ready up whoever is done for the day by holding out their backpacks and making sure they're not crying, or bleeding, or something along those lines before mom or dad sees them.

Though we don't talk much, I can at least recognize most of the parents. This woman has never been here before, I'm sure of it. And she looks like my past.

Minutes pass and I'm standing behind the check-in table now. I can't seem to think about anything else. Alice is beside me, fumbling over a pen that is running out of ink. She keeps scribbling on the back of an old grocery receipt she found in her purse instead of picking up a new pen from the old mug we use as a pencil holder on the crafts table three feet away.

"How come you've never asked me about my family?" I ask Alice suddenly. It's more accusing than I mean for it to be, but there it is. "You ask everyone else. *What are you doing this weekend, Bradley? Visiting your parents again, Rosa? How's your sister doing, Quinn?*" I do a hip shake with each poor Alice impersonation.

The clipboard clatters in a louder thunk than I intend, though I am already walking out the door, mumbling to no one in particular that I need a moment.

She's beside me after what feels like a long time, but really only a few breaths. Enough for me to already feel ashamed for the outburst. I swear, I'm not normally like this.

"I'm sorry," I start. "I'm in a rough patch, and I can't seem to get over it."

She asks me if I want to talk about it. I think I scoff.

"I know you think I'm an odd nut," adds Alice. "But I'm a good listener."

"Just do me a favor," I say.

"What's that?" she asks.

"Don't offer me any advice."

Silent nods of agreement from the both of us, and here I am. About to spill my guts like a free-of-charge therapy session, and I don't want to tell Alice about you. I don't want to talk about Hannah, or even Mitchell. I know the mother who just walks in doesn't actually look like her, but it's something about her put-togetherness. I want to tell Alice about Mrs. Neza.

~

Hannah was away on vacation. Meeting a long-time friend who was in Santa Barbara for the weekend. It wasn't something that happened often. She hardly took days off from work, let alone went on vacation.

In the world of foster care, that means a temporary home. Usually, people testing out the whole foster parent thing. We were lucky, as we always like to say we are, and the social worker managed to keep us together once more for this extra temporary stay with the Nezas during the two days Hannah was gone.

The Neza home was lovely, or so it seemed in my almost-a-tween, not-very-design-oriented, fairly simple mind. The outside was painted a warm cream color and the roof was a shade of brown that reminded me of milk chocolate. The whole house was dressed in matching furniture, all in either a deep blue, light brown, or a yellow. Even the hand towels in the bathroom and the bed sheets we were given to make the twin bed and pull-out mattress where we'd be staying were of the same color scheme.

Jerry Neza was a delight. He had the kind of energy Mitchell and I only had combined on a good day. Jerry must have been a little older than me, a little younger than Mitchell.

I still remember him; he talked fast and loved race cars and had a bunch of toy figures stacked on top of one another on the shelves hanging over his bed. His plastic bedframe was shaped like a race car and had a real door that swung open for him to get in and everything. He was always coming up with storylines for us to act out and pretend. Mitchell, who was getting too old for pretend apparently, mostly ignored him. I followed him everywhere.

Mrs. Neza was kind enough. She interested me in the way older, beautiful women interest young girls on the brink of puberty. I remember forcing myself to turn away from where her high heels were stashed by the door, or from her lace bras resting in the laundry basket she left on the living room couch. I'd blush every time, then get back to running around the house with Jerry or Mitchell. The Neza residence was a new playground for me, and Jerry was a great guide for the ways of carefree childhoods.

There was a treehouse in their backyard that Jerry told us Mr. Neza built for him over last Thanksgiving break. It was just a few pieces of wood nailed together, no makeshift roof of any sort, but I never saw anything grander in my life. All I could think about during our stay was getting to the top of that treehouse.

Jerry, to my disappointment, was over the treehouse by the time I came along. He found his new YuGiOh cards much more interesting. And Jerry, once again to my disappointment, wasn't one for compromise. Especially when it came to playtime.

It was a late afternoon, an hour or so after school. Mrs. Neza left a snack out for us on the kitchen counter: celery with little individual peanut butter dip cups, string cheese, and homemade lemonade already poured into three paper cups. Mom-business was very important to Mrs. Neza. She told us that for the second time since we arrived. She thought that was such a hilarious phrase, "mom-business."

We finished the food, taking our time, as kids do sometimes. Mitchell threw away the trash and scraps left on the counter while Jerry recruited me to help him look for one of his missing YuGiOh cards—he swore he left it in the living room. Mrs. Neza was out of sight by now, but she was home, she must have been. She took naps in her bedroom, never the couch.

I could feel Mitchell rolling his eyes behind me as Jerry's anxiety rose. As Jerry remembered how important this one particular card was. *Homebound kids*, Mitchell would have said if he had the chance.

Mitchell never left his stuff in the living room, even at Hannah's. He never got out of the habit of keeping all of his belongings close and within eyesight until sometime around his high school years. *So you don't forget it when you leave* most of the foster parents said, or so I've heard from our own temporary kids.

They usually wanted to go, that's what Hannah told us. They were older kids, ones who remembered their parents, or usually still lived with their real families until the next time trouble appeared. They'd take care of them, of their troubled parents, they'd all say, itching to get out of Hannah's house. They needed to get back.

We searched for the card for about fifteen minutes, and Jerry was growing more and more impatient. We only took one break—a concentration record for Jerry—during which he showed me a fresh cut on his cheek from school yesterday and tried to pull the crusty skin around it outwards to make the scar larger.

"You didn't see it anywhere?" Jerry asked me for about the tenth time, pushing the couch cushions from side to side and checking beneath each.

"Actually, I think I remember seeing it outside," I said.

Now Jerry turned toward me. Narrowed his eyes. "Outside?" he asked.

"In the treehouse," I said with a nod.

"That's stupid. How would it have gotten all the way up to the treehouse?"

"I put it there," I said.

"You wouldn't," said Jerry. "You're too much of a scaredy-cat."

"Only one way to find out," I smiled innocently and pushed open the sliding door with one hand.

"If I take you up there," Jerry said with a sigh. "Will you tell me where you put it already?"

I nodded, pulling the rope ladder down for Jerry to lead the way.

Excitement shot through my legs, my toes, my fingers. Jerry got up to the top and sat himself upright on the narrow wooden floors, and I didn't wince when he grabbed my arm and pulled me up impatiently.

Nothing seemed like it could be dangerous, of course. We liked bouncing on the soft spot of the wood and laughed at the creaking sound it made. The fall was a two-part fall. First, I curled back into a strange position, just slightly over the edge of the treehouse flooring and the branch of the tree. For a minute I just hung there, understanding that I couldn't pull myself out of this. Part two was the full fall down to the ground. Quick, swift. Once on the ground, I tried to roll or crawl back into the last position I was in, as if I get a redo. I don't remember the tears starting, they were just there.

I rolled my head back and Mrs. Neza was already there, as if she'd been watching us play out in the backyard all this time. She pushed me aside and held each of Jerry's arms out, flipped his palms back and forth, pulled his trousers up to check his legs. She fretted over the cut on his cheek for a while, the one he tried to pull into a larger scar earlier.

Mitchell trailed after Mrs. Neza when the big thunk of the tree branch sounded. After sending him off to get Neosporin from the top shelf of the kitchen cabinet, Mrs. Neza pulled me up to a sitting position and checked me for scratches, placed bandages where I was bleeding. We all went back inside and Mrs. Neza gave Jerry a ring pop. Locked the cabinet.

I must have said something about it, or sighed enough times for Mrs. Neza to notice, because I remember her sighing back at me and saying, "Jerry's my only son. Only sons and daughters get spoiled."

Or was it, "real son?" "Real child?"

Maybe that's what she said. I used to swear that I remember the wording, but you know how memory works. Always altered and a little torn up, scarred from time. This is what I remember, this is the one that stuck: *I'll always pick my child before you. My real one. Always.*

Of course, I want to say to Mrs. Neza now, *of course flesh and blood comes first, always.* The whole situation was titled temporary—temporary stay, temporary, temporary—until Hannah got back from her trip. But were we temporaries there, too? I tried to imagine what Hannah would do if she saw Jerry and I fall from the tree.

Still, Mrs. Neza was the monster that day who tore apart a little piece of my youthful self-esteem and shone a light on a world I knew so well. A direct statement of your secondary importance is a peculiar thing. You realize how all of us naturally assume importance. To be a priority, even when we know it's ridiculous.

Later, with Alice, I do what I did then. I hold my breath and count to five, something a nurse from urgent care taught me to do after the fall to keep from crying. Hannah took me there after she picked us up, just to make sure all was alright. My lower back still hurt from the fall.

The nurse's skin seemed dusted with glitter, like pearls dropped in sand, and I remember her touch was the sort of cold that didn't make you shiver. After taking my blood pressure and listening to my heart, the nurse explained life to me by holding up two very important things: a reflex hammer and a drinking straw. She pointed to the base of the reflex hammer, pinched the straw between her index finger and thumb, then looked at me.

"Both of these things are made out of plastic," she said. "You have muscles and bones, just like any other girl."

I nodded.

"But because of how your body works, a little differently." She bent the straw and twisted it twice. "Some of your bones are more delicate than others."

Then came the X-rays and she ruffled my hair the way older siblings always do in TV shows and told me that I'm stronger than just bones.

I'm not afraid of finding you, I'm not afraid, I'm not. And if I do turn out to be, I won't let silly feelings like being scared ruin me. I'm made out of more substance than that.

Alice keeps her promise. She doesn't even ask any questions. I wonder if she's even interested. Even listening? She stands next to me and sighs deeply. Our breath becomes exactly in tune, so much so that we could be just one loud breather.

"When I was eighteen, I was so sure I had my life planned out," starts Alice. "I'm a fantastic sprinter. I don't say it to brag, it's just the truth. I thought for sure the Olympics, and then coaching at Stanford, like my brother was doing. It was the only thing I was ever really good at." We stand quietly for a while. "Most of the stuff that happen to us in our lives won't really make any sense to us. We meet people who make a lasting impression, and then never see them again. We make plans for the future, and everything falls apart. The point isn't actually what happens, or even what we decide to do about it. It's how we do it. It's why."

Eventually I ask her. *Why? Why here? Why this?*

"I love the kids. They have so much spirit. I think every inch of the world could use a little bit more spirit. Do you know what I mean?"

"Sure. I guess so," I murmur. It dawns on me that Alice seems calm. I don't think I've ever seen her this way. I like it.

Next, I lie. I say I haven't even thought about finding you. *What's the point?* is my answer. *Maybe you'll find out once you see her,* is hers.

Chapter Twelve: Charlotte

Keeping our hands busy, bumping shoulders while standing beside each other in loose jeans and old sweatshirts is the exact sort of thing I need for the chance to look at my mother. Really look at her. The blue in her eyes thickened over the years, her skin freckled and her cheeks pinched. She's smaller, somehow, and more present. She searches the light brown rug for the duct tape she let drop someplace and laughs when she gets her foot trapped in an empty cardboard box.

The move sets Mom off on a cleaning/sorting/throwing out/donating sort of mood, so that's exactly what we've been doing with all of our time ever since the going away party.

She shoves a cardboard box into my hands. "When in doubt, throw it away," she says as she tries to tear a piece of tape off the roll with her teeth.

Once we've gotten into a rhythm of organizing and categorizing, she fills the silence by asking me questions she's never asked before.

"I want to know all about your life abroad," she says. "Don't leave anything out."

"You know all about it," I say. "It's not like we never spoke."

It was phone calls every few Sundays at the beginning. Sundays were usually when we docked, and when I remembered to, I tried to call. Emails were better, but made for more room. It became difficult to fill the empty space, guessing what they'd like to hear. So I called. It was laborious. One day, when I was talking to my father and I could hear him trying not to chew too loudly with a bunch of distant voices in the background, it became clear that they didn't know what to say either. I stopped calling unless I had something to say.

Mom blinks at me expectantly. No, hopefully. In a way that makes me embarrassed for her. I shrug.

"We switched off on stops every few months," I start. "It all depended. But for the most part, each cruise was a week at a time, different stops throughout the Caribbean." Another shrug. "Then we'd do it all over again."

More timid questions. *But where, and how did you get around, and what did you need to know, a woman traveling all alone, by herself. A young woman.*

She grills me for city names, and whether local buses or train schedules were best to navigate, and how I made sure not to get gypped when exchanging currency. I realize our lives just swapped.

I tell her the good stuff. Skip over the long hours, the shared cabins with the beds we'd share (or swap, rather) with people from different shifts, the anonymity, the mundane. I tell her about the places we went to with both mountain and ocean views, about getting lost among street signs in languages we didn't understand, but not worrying because we were told feeling different and out of place was normal when you're a tourist.

"The Cayman Islands, Jamaica, Dominican Republic, sure." I nod after she guesses a couple of spots. "We went to all of them eventually."

"What an adventure of a life you had," she finally says. Her eyes are sparkling. I sigh.

"Did you have fun on Friday, dear?" she asks suddenly.

I dig deeper past an old sleeping bag and a pile of old dish towels into the back of her closet.

"Huh? Oh yeah," I say. "You sure were getting your groove on."

She chuckles with me and I swear I see her blush. My mother blushes?

"I'm sorry if I embarrassed you," she says. "You probably didn't expect to come home and find me so loopy."

"It's fine, I get it. Getting ready for your big excursion and all. European nights, European men, European wines."

"Believe it or not, that's not what this trip is about."

"Oh, really? What is it about then?" I ask.

"Making up for lost time. God knows, it is time I had some adventure in my life. We old folks can do that, you know. Keep living." Mom smirks at me as she places a strip of tape on the last of the boxes for donation. At least the last from this room. The study, the living room, and the kitchen still need to be raided.

Aside from her neatly made bed, a sparse dresser, and some now naked nails on the walls, the room my parents shared for most nights of their lives is empty.

"I feel like I just shed fifty pounds. You should do your room next," Mom says to me.

~

"You're so quiet," he said to me.

"I'm not," I replied. "Just nervous, I guess. Are you sure about this guy?"

"Trust me, Charlie," Keith said. "Just trust me."

A suspended Tamagotchi keychain swayed between us from the rear-view mirror of Keith's Ford Explorer. Outside the passenger window stood a warm winter day. I was shivering, and the A/C was going. Something sweet and syrupy was in the air, like cinnamon roll crumbs or something else just barely there. *I miss him* I said in my head and started to tear up. Keith must have noticed and thought I was chickening out.

"This is his job," Keith said. "He knows what he's doing."

"And then everything can go back to normal. Right?"

"Yeah. Like nothing ever happened."

~

The practitioner was a loud and angry man. He'd pace the room, carelessly tossing his equipment about with clanks that made me jump, complaining about how late Keith and I arrived to our appointment. Keith told me he was the only person who treated women in their third trimesters, so there we were.

I'm not saying that I didn't know that it was illegal. I knew. But so was littering. So was drinking when you were under twenty-one. So was parking in the handicapped spot when you didn't need it.

"How long is this going to take?" asked Keith.

"About an hour, give or take," answered the practitioner. "Then I'll have you two back here in about fourteen hours, or whenever you start feeling labor pain."

Keith sighed. I laid my head back on the hospital bed and listened intently to the steady rhythm of the machinery as if nothing else in the universe mattered, or even existed at that moment. My head was throbbing and my insides felt as if they were burning. I tried so hard not to think. Your heartbeat was pounding, what kind of place would want me to listen to your heartbeat before you go?

I must have been tense, because every time he touched me, it hurt. Incredible, sporadic shocks of stinging, pressing, my body shaking and begging to be left alone sort of pain. Maybe we should have listened.

I still remember how the practitioner froze.

"What is it?" Keith asked.

The practitioner cursed. "She's going into labor," he said.

"What?" asked Keith.

"It's phase one of the abortion. Delivery happens during phase two. It's too soon."

"Already?"

"I'm going to have to deliver," said the practitioner, with a sigh.

I knew it the moment that it happened. My insides continued to burn, a buzzing built in my ear that still visits me sometimes, my vision was all blurry. Something was terribly wrong.

Jaw set tight, I tried my best not to let my eyes focus again, to step into the dizziness. I wanted the blurriness to stay with me. I thought it'd be more bearable that way. I closed my eyes, but it didn't help. The pain was everywhere.

The swearing continued. I no longer knew if it was the practitioner, or Keith, or elsewhere, and I didn't care. I no longer cared. I just wanted out. A reset. Some mercy.

I heard you shriek for the first time, and the room cleared. The practitioner said something about consequences. How the salt saline made you brittle. That this has happened before, in the past, just not to him. That survivors lived, they lived just fine. That things like this happen.

He was holding you when he asked Keith something, packed his things incredibly fast and left after that. I lay there with my arms circled as if I were holding you, still looking up at the ceiling and waiting. I'm not sure when Keith left, but I took the bus home by myself. Don't ask me how I pulled that off. I can't even remember walking out the door.

What do you want me to say? That my intentions were never to harm you? That I've regret your almost death every single day of my life since the moment I saw your little face, darkened with shades of pinks and blues, gasping for its first gulp of air?

All I know for sure is that I stopped being angry with my parents the moment I let go of you. I wanted to give you the best chance that I could. That was the unspoken reason for them, I knew. We all believe in different versions of a best chance. Who's to say who's right?

~

I came home with drying blood on my clothes and slammed the brakes on my parents when I explained to them that we wouldn't need a doctor, not anymore.

After my mother cried and my father told me that I had sinned, I wept through two pillowcases and stole away late at night to the BART station. An overwhelming desire to watch the sunrise in San Francisco took control.

After the hour-long train ride, burrowing deep within my oversized coat, I sat at a park at the top of a hill. There was a water view and the wind directed fierce blows at my bare ears. The night sky was magnificent–it was the first time I saw a cloud from its side without flying through it. Some people say standing so high makes you feel small, but I preferred to let the massiveness of it all seep into me. My fingertips tingled, mistakenly believing to have the power to move anything below me if I pleased. I fixated on the clouds. They floated aimlessly, unruffled by the clamminess of the city sky, stretching into neat layers within each other, and began to color. The sun was coming. Lavenders, deep purples, light blues and darks alike, pale yellows, oranges that burst—those were my favorite. As the light began to scatter, it became clear that there was too much fog rolling about to draw a line between what is sky and what is ocean, and it was best that way.

When we haven't experienced much yet, when we step back and observe a moment, we expect it to look the way it would in a coloring book. Orderly, within respective lines, blank at its beginning and finished when it's finished. It's not true. Making a mess is so much more beautiful. The sun was a perfectly round circle at first, but now the rays extended and retracted in staggering rhythms. No beginning and no end, even when it found a certain height in the sky that we train ourselves to believe is up and in place. Only pulses and measures.

Prayer drifted out of me forever that morning, at least the type of prayer I was used to. Ever since I got pregnant, I felt too frightened, too guilty, too heavy to ask God for anything. But praying to the sunrays or the grass or the trees, that was light.

Time passed, but it was okay because it passed gently, and I could see absolutely everything from where I stood.

Chapter Thirteen: Evie

Do you remember the first time you swam all by yourself? The moment right before your instructor let go, and even though their hands still hovered over you, your heart was racing and your breath quickened and you still just weren't old enough to fully understand if it was fear or excitement you were feeling, or how it was possible to juggle two opposites like that at the same time?

I do. I remember. I remember how I was both relieved and a little hurt that Hannah kept me swimming on the rug instead of inside the water for so long. She would have me swimming on the floor forever as long as it was up to her, I realized one day. Hoping I'd get bored and move on to some other pastime, forget all about the arm stroke memory game that we played—her yelling out *butterfly* or *backstroke*, me wiggling and contorting on the carpet.

That's what I must have been thinking of that day when, four years after my first floor stroke lesson, I dipped my toe in the water, and Mitchell told me no, and I welcomed the incredibly cold water on my rug burned skin, unsure if it would hold me up or pull me down till this swimming business was washed out of me.

In retrospect, digging up this memory of mine was my first mistake. It's our fifth day of swim lessons. Jessie still tenses up whenever I hold her just barely over the shallow end. I have her swim on a foam boogie board that is too small for her, her arms and legs flopping off the ends like noodles. I decide this is better than a rug.

My new morning ritual includes a reminder to put all of me into teaching Jessie how to swim. It's something I think I can do almost flawlessly. I don't want to think about anything else.

Yet disappointment washes over me when Jessie walks in this particular morning. She looks like hell. She unzips her backpack with the fire truck on the front and throws her swim clothes on the floor with angry huffs, and doesn't want to swim. She doesn't look at anyone besides her dad.

"What's wrong?" I ask.

"We're having a bad morning," Jessie's father says plainly.

She starts whimpering when her dad scoops her up into his calm arms and whispers in her ear with kisses. It doesn't help. She tries to wiggle her way loose.

"I just need you to take her," he says to me finally, and places Jessie in my arms. Her cries are unnaturally loud, and her eyes are dry.

I stand awkwardly with Jessie in my outstretched arms. "We'll be in the far-right lane," I say to Jessie's father in case he wants to stay and watch.

The two left lanes are always reserved for group swims, where the rest of the kids will be. The middle to the public, ours I claimed for private lessons.

He nods a quick goodbye to me and heads back to his car, hunching his shoulders in the tight way that lets us know he doesn't intend to look back.

Jessie stares up at me. *I'm in charge. Right.*

I let Jessie put her feet in the water as I go through different arm movements. From now on she's very attentive. We don't use the Minnie Mouse floaties Jessie's dad keeps bringing along to every lesson, even though I've already told him that floaties are against pool rules. Choking hazard. I hover over her for every second of the swim.

It's noisy today, making it hard for me to hear her, but Jessie is blabbering non-stop. Something about a carnival and Hawaiian potato chips.

Noise is the new normal around here. The place is turning into a theme park of sorts, management's attempt to stay competitive. Weekly family pool parties and musical cardio exercises for all ages in the pool. We recently opened up a bouncy room, and of course, our prized possession: the largest indoor climbing wall in the state. There are even talks of an indoor sky-diving station coming soon.

We spend about fifteen minutes swimming back and forth across the width of the shallow end of the pool.

"Great work," I say after a fierce doggy paddle from Jess.

"More!" Jess slaps her palms up and down against the water in happy splashes.

It happens fast. Some kid grabs a handful of Jess's hair and pulls her down with him. Lifeguard jumps in. It's only then I realize Jessie is completely underwater. Stuck under that boy's hand.

Everyone else in the pool politely looks away but keeps quiet to let me know they are still watching and that I'm an idiot.

The lifeguard hands Jess over to one of the other instructors, some high schooler who happens to be on break and comes over to check what the racket is about. She wraps Jess up in one of the pool's plain white towels and tucks the edge in like a straitjacket. Burrito-style, as the kids called it.

Jessie doesn't cry. She doesn't complain. She furrows her eyebrows. She does that more than any other four-year-old I've ever met.

Tall for her age, I can tell she's going to grow up to be insanely beautiful, the kind that makes strangers jealous. I get her apple juice from the staff room and she seems happy with that.

"Peek-a-boo," Alice says, sneaking up behind me.

"Jesus, Alice." I sigh. "Are you here to check on Jessie?"

"Yes. And you."

"Lifeguard told you?"

Alice nods. She tickles Jessie until she gets a good laugh and turns back to me. "Failure is important," she starts. "Don't you think so?"

I raise an eyebrow.

"Oh, don't make everything into such a drama. Saving shouldn't be a drama." Alice gives me her closed-mouth smile. "For example, coffee and *The Morning Show* save me. They are comforting. Comfort is so important."

"You know you sound like a fortune cookie."

"Watch it," she says. "I am still your boss."

We smile at each other. Noticing her graying bangs for the first time, I realize she's much older than I imagined. She's managed to maintain that I-will-save-the-world youthful thing most people shed.

She removes the lanyard holding all the keys to the building from her neck and wraps it around her palm a few times as she starts toward the door. "And stop worrying already," she adds. "It's a useless state."

"And how do you suppose I manage that?" I ask.

"Presence," she responds.

"What the hell does that mean?" I ask. "Oh, I get it. My job is just to be, is that it?"

"Don't roll your eyes, Evie. And no, not quite. Be present, not perfect."

I sigh.

"It means, you smartass, you'll be happier once you just let things slide. So today sucked. Let it go. You'll wear yourself out otherwise, fighting yourself all the time," Alice says.

Did Alice just say smartass?

"I have no idea who you are anymore," I start. It's then that Jessie's dad arrives.

He swings her swim bag over one of his shoulders and helps her pull her hair back into a neat, high ponytail. They walk over to me and Jess gives me a hug to let me know that she's leaving now. Same as always. But he has that we-need-to-have-a-chat face on.

"Let me know if you need me," Alice says quietly with a supportive squeeze of the shoulder before leaving me with the sign-out clipboard.

"I'm sorry," I begin before Jessie's dad can say anything. "I thought I had her."

He looks confused. So does Jess.

"Tomorrow," Jess says to me. "Can we play with the diving toys like the big kids?"

"You got it," I say only a beat too late. I hand the clipboard over to her dad.

Jess's dad whispers something to Jess and she skips away toward the café happily with a ten-dollar bill in her hand.

"Look this isn't easy to say, so I'm just going to come right out with it," he says to me. "Jess's mother and I are getting a divorce. Probably. Jess accidentally heard us talking about it. She doesn't understand why I'm moving out." He sighs. "So anyways, I know that she's upset and moodier than usual, and I appreciate your patience and the distraction, your work with her in the pool. Gives her time to focus on something else for a while. It's real important to us."

"What?" I blurt out. He looks surprised. Then embarrassed. I feel terrible for both of those reactions. "Oh. I understand." I put a hand on his

133

arm. He looks down at it as if I placed something lethal there. *Okay, Evie. Retract. Retract.*

I clasp my hands together in front of my chest and rock back on my heels. "Divorce can be tough," I say.

"Right," he pauses for a while and stares off. "Are you married?"

I'm caught off guard by the question. I must react somehow, because he gives me that gorgeous smile and says, "I'm sorry, I shouldn't have asked that. You're so young. It's none of my business. It's just so different from what you always imagine it to be like."

"Marriage?"

"Everything," he says. Not sadly, just matter-of-fact like. I'm not sure that I prefer this.

"Got everything, kiddo?" he says to Jessie. She's trailing, dragging her jean jacket behind her with a smirk that says she ate too much chocolate while saying her goodbyes to the rest of the staff.

"Anyways, I'm so sorry if I overshared." He looks back at me now. "I just figured, you and Jess will be spending a lot of time together and I want you to know where all of this—" He waves his arm around. "Is coming from." He leans in and says a little quieter. "She usually is a sweet and easy kid."

"I get it. I'm glad you told me."

We talk a bit more about swimming, about the weekend, about a birthday party Jessie got invited to today. Her father stares at the invitation with a frown on his face.

"I don't know, kiddo," he says. "Maybe we can find you a carpool," he mumbles again.

"If you need help driving the kids around in the meantime, I'm happy to help," I hear myself saying. "Until things settle down."

Wait, what?

"I couldn't ask you to do that." He shakes his head.

"I did offer," I respond.

"I suppose we could pay you what you make here by the hour. Make it worth your time. How does that sound?"

We nod, we exchange phone numbers. We say our final goodbyes, yet again, and here I am, left wondering what the hell I think I'm doing. Between two jobs, when will I possibly find the time to chauffeur these kids around? Didn't I already decide a third job was a bad idea?

Something like horrified amusement washes over me as I toss some swim towels in the wash and gently pull my heart strings back one by one from where they've fallen deep inside of my stomach. *Divorce, huh?* Remembering Jessie's redhead mother passing out kisses in the minivan, I just don't think that it can be.

~

The rest of the day is unnaturally long, and I can't stop stealing glances at the clock during the late afternoon session. I stand and stare silently as the kids entertain themselves with a couple of foam balls and stuffed animals, and when my knee starts to hurt, I remove my red and black rain boots and sit on the rug with my legs stretched outward in a V.

Will bear crawls over to me and collapses on my shins.

"I want to be a tarantula," he says, arms flung over his head, eyes wide and upwards and not seeing the ceiling.

"Do you like tarantulas?" he asks me.

"Nope."

"You should."

"And why is that?" I ask.

"Why wouldn't you like tarantulas?"

"Most people are scared of tarantulas, Will. They're dangerous."

"I like being scared," he says and sits up.

"No, you don't. Nobody *likes* being afraid."

He loses interest and digs his little feet into my boots. Half of him disappears into the large polka-dot print rubber and I feel big and old.

"How many days until May fifth?" he asks.

"Six."

"That's my birthday. I'm getting a pet tarantula and I'm going to name him Phil. And I'm getting a turtle. But I'm not going to put them together or else they'll fight and I don't want Phil to lose one of his legs."

"Good thinking," I say.

"When's your birthday?" Will asks me with sweet eyes. He's looking up at me and for the first time he looks like he's actually paying attention.

Do you know how much it kills me to realize that I can't even confidently answer such a basic question anymore? I know what day the state received custody of me. My birthday. But was it? How long between the panic of my birth and the moment we separated for good? Hours, days, weeks?

"You should get a tarantula, Evie," continues Will. Never mind on the paying attention thing. "If you get a tarantula, you'll take care of it and you won't be scared of it anymore. And then Phil will have a girlfriend."

He crawls away and I stay seated in my listless state, thinking about everything that happened today. Perhaps I've been too hard on Alice, this woman who knew exactly what I needed when she told me to teach Jessie how to swim.

Do I really have to go away to resolve this? Can't I just go back to normal? Rain boots were made to keep us dry, being dry is safe and good, I want to be safe and good, maybe it's best we stay away from each other, maybe one of us is the turtle attacking the tarantula, maybe I should just forget it, grab some takeout for dinner and talk of nothing but the weather and traffic tonight with Mitchell, maybe, maybe, maybe.

~

Neither of us have much energy left in us when we decide to go looking for you. For real this time.

Each of our own long days knocked the wind out of us. It's evening and Mitchell and I are both staring at the *Food Network* playing on TV. Neither of us are remotely close to sitting up straight. Eventually one of us will probably slip off the couch. We do not speak much tonight the way we usually do. It must be funny to you, to anyone on the outside looking in, how these two childhood friends who still live together resemble an old couple glued to the couch.

"I'm so tired of it, Mitch," I say into our mostly empty living room. "I'm tired of my new life."

"What are you talking about?" he asks.

I tell him about my day. About swim lessons, about daycare, about divorce, about watching Jessie almost drown. About laughing with Alice, about birthdays, about tarantulas.

"Do you think it's normal how hooked you get on these families?"

"I know. It's super weird." I scratch my head. Scratch my elbows, scratch my back. Suddenly, I cannot sit still. "I'm just sad for them. Everyone gets divorced eventually, don't they?"

"You're upset about strangers. Strangers that aren't perfect enough for you."

"What?" I start. "They aren't strangers—"

"And that there isn't a perfect family out there for you." The words are harsh. But Mitchell doesn't sound malicious.

"Maybe I shouldn't have recommended Alice to you," he continues. "Maybe you should try to forget."

I shake my head.

These are some facts, this is what I know: Octopus blood is blue. Blue whales are the loudest animals in the world. Shrimp carry their heart in their heads. It happens faster than you think it will;

one day you wake up and realize you haven't thought about your disappointments the way you used to. You get tired of obsessing. You hardly think about it at all, and it doesn't burn so much when you do. But you and I, us, our ties, our history. That was never an obsession for me. It was a shock. It's a story burdening me, thrust upon me. I must find you to get an ending I can live with.

"Let's go on a road trip," I say slowly.

"Really?" For the first time today, Mitchell doesn't sound drained.

"Let's go. I'm tired of pretending. Or waiting. Or whatever the hell I've been doing these days." I shrug a big shrug. It helps begin to loosen a knot in my shoulders. "Will you help me look for answers?"

Of course he will.

Conversation buzzes in our little home yet again as we each look at the map on our phones and try to plan a last-minute trip without understanding the destination. We turn off the *Food Network*, share a beer, and both call it a night by ten p.m.

Chapter Fourteen: Charlotte

This is what happened back then. Before me, after you.

I left home for the seas at twenty-three. The ship was my home seven days a week, with few breaks—all spent sleeping. During my first gig, we left at ten a.m. every Saturday of every week. We began preparing rooms and the common areas at four a.m. The late mornings were used to carry luggage with the occasional tip, change the white cotton bed sheets, polish the marble hallway floors, save sad smiles for seeing people out the door and happy smiles for greeting new guests.

Things were a little different at sea than I had expected. Each staff dormitory had two bunk beds that hung off the walls instead of on wooden legs. These were called our quad rooms. When I stood in the middle and spread both of my arms out, I could almost touch both walls at once.

Most weeks looked the same. Four women rolling out of the staggered beds that dangle off the walls like coat hooks, changing into matching white and green polo shirts and khaki pants, fighting sleep as gentle winds swayed the ship into a lullaby.

Pulling their hair back into buns or braids while walking to their morning shifts at the buffet and it's still dark out, trying so hard to catch and caress the lingering minutes spent so well in silence before clocking in.

We traded off on tasks, sometimes setting the hundreds of tables before the guests flooded in, sometimes unloading the dishwasher. Then we'd each pick a spot for the six a.m. opening, either behind a serving counter or at the front door welcoming guests and passing out hand sanitizer. As people ate, I'd move on to the gym and wipe down the equipment from sweat stains. Then I'd either vacuum or serve in the café, depending on the day, nap for an hour and a half, change into my evening uniform (basically the same thing, but a shortened skirt instead of khakis), head over to the sports bar and work until the last of the customers went to bed.

I thought I was signing up for a wild adventure, but I hardly ever got a chance to get off the ship.

Mop the ballroom floors. Vacuum rooms 228 to 310. Set the buffet tables. Wash and dry the silverware. Mop the ballroom floors. Vacuum rooms 311 to 347. Set the buffet tables. Wash and dry the silverware.

My life was boring. The work was hard. I was surrounded by coworkers who wished they were at home with their families. And I was digging, scrubbing, sprinting, doing absolutely anything and everything I could to get away from mine, to get away from you.

I eventually was transferred over to a new Caribbean cruise line, and life remained mostly the same. One time I got off with all the tourists at Ochos Rios, Jamaica for almost a full day. I remember that morning very well because I got my largest tip ever—twenty dollars—when I remembered the same woman I served the day before liked her morning tea with honey and soy milk.

I was by myself walking the colorful streets of seaside Jamaica, dresses of thin fabric and white button-up shirts hanging out from the multi-story apartment building windows to dry, docking ships ringing, taxi drivers yelling things like "No worries" and "Sir, where you going, sir" at every passer-byer, my wavy hair frizzing in the damp heat.

I heard a teenage boy walking the streets a few strides in front of me say, "Dunn's River Falls. It's the Eiffel tower of Jamaica." So I went there. Nothing like the Eiffel tower in my mind, but certainly the widest waterfall I'd ever seen.

The air tasted like tap water mixed with sugar, and the ground was rocky and hurt my heels through my thin sandals. I rented black waterproof shoes from the information desk where there was a sign that said, "No Open-Toe Shoes Allowed," and the teenage girl at the counter told me to walk downhill until I saw a group of people wearing blue vests.

There were lots of families, a few retired folks, a few couples. It felt so strange being the only one not traveling with someone else to talk to and yet being surrounded by so much noise. I began to feel self-conscious. Like everyone was staring at me, everyone roaring, the bright colored island I fell in love with just moments earlier focusing in on me like bullets at attention, even the river stream demanding, *she is alone* they'd say *she is the only lonely being here and it's her own damn fault.*

I found the group tour at the bottom of the hill, as promised. Our guide's name was Tim. He was tall and carried a video camera with him the whole way up and had the group, about thirty of us, smile and yell "Ya, man!" at him before getting into a straight line. We were going to walk up the waterfall. Tim told us to hold hands and, for heaven's sake, not to let go and try to take a shortcut.

It's wrong, walking up instead of down the way the water spills. That's why I liked it. It seemed significant. It seemed bizarre. It seemed off the beaten path. It seemed like something I would do.

We began on the sliver of dirt bordering the stream, dodging the fallen tree branches and still holding each other's hands. There was a fast, small girl in front of me, probably about nine years old, and a middle-aged man followed by his wife behind me. Finally, Tim led us between two big rocks and into the water itself, about one and a half feet deep, pebbly and lukewarm. A single flip-flop floated past me.

Tim was a serious guy, but I could tell he loved the kids the best. "Be careful of River Mumma," he said as the young Americans in the group squirmed away from their parents and ran ahead to where Tim walked barefoot.

"You all have Cinderella and her glass slipper." Tim stomped his foot twice, ran his fingers through the water surface and splashed the front of the line. "We have River Mumma."

"River Mumma?"

Tim continued, rubbing his large palms together and sighing, knowing he had all of our ears now by the growing hush of the water stream below us. "She is Jamaica's oldest legend. She is the woman of the river. A beautiful one, and a tricky one. They say she leaves a golden jeweled comb on rocks by the shore to tempt people. Once someone picks up the comb, she drags him into the river to drown."

"Why?" asked one of the kids.

"So we learn not to be so greedy," Tim said. "The river belongs to her. Even eating the fish from the river should be avoided because they are her children and no one wants an angry River Mumma. Many people say they have seen her sitting on these rocks, combing her hair. Or at least they used to say that, back when the Spanish first came to Jamaica and told this story all of the time."

"Why did Spanish people come here?" another one of the kids running between Tim's large steps asked. The kid's blonde hair was half wet, half dry, standing straight up at the ends like a scarecrow.

"For gold." Tim laughed. "The weird thing is some people say her hair is dark brown. Some say it is blue." He shrugged. "So she is beautiful, she is dangerous, and that's why Jamaicans would bring her gifts whenever they'd have to cross the river. Tried to seduce her back."

"Did it work?" The same little boy with the dirty blonde hair asked.

"I've walked up this river eighty-seven times." He winked at the boy. "Haven't been dragged nowhere by some woman yet."

Looking down, I noticed some blood sprinkling across my knee. I must have brushed by one of the tall rocks near the river and cut myself earlier while Tim spoke. It started to sting. I splashed some water on it and lowered myself down on a dry dirt patch to sit. We got the okay to let go of each other's hands because we were at the top now. Not actually the top of the waterfall, but the highest spot we were allowed to go to. I made sure not to step on any of the river's fish.

It was a gorgeous view. The waterfall rushing into the ocean. Looking down on the path we hiked up was like realizing that every twig, or leaf, or color reflected on the river surface was out of place until now. An intimate skim of a detail, a single ingredient, a puzzle piece only now serving its purpose in the giant portrait hanging beneath us. The reward.

I tried to breathe in loudly, only because I'd been quiet for so long and it bothered me. It was already time to go back to the ship.

I gave Tim the twenty-dollar tip I received earlier, readjusted the heel of my waterproof shoe, and wondered what the heck I was doing here.

~

"I want you to stay," she says, zipping up her black carry-on with her wrists and thumbs for the final time this evening. Her left hand is interlaced with a yellow mug full to the brim with hot tea, her right is busy clutching her cell phone charger. "This is our home. You should take care of it while I'm gone. I'd like you to."

"You told me this was just to help you pack up the place, Mom," I say. "I thought your agent already found some family that was interested in the house. Isn't that what you told me?"

Of course it was, but that's never the point.

"I want you to stay," he said. I was quitting. I was leaving. I had to.

I thought I had nothing more to say, so he did all the talking.

"Could we at least discuss this before you do something crazy?" And then in a quieter voice: "Is this about what I said yesterday? You're scared, aren't you?"

"You're scared, aren't you?" she says, tilting her head at me. She's so different now, but she sees me just the same. "This town. It won't hurt you, you know."

"I won't hurt you, you know." I hated it when he said that. He said it all of the time.

Most things about the two of us I didn't actually hate. There were things I already missed. Getting sesame bagels and decaf coffee for him with cream

and no sugar, a chai tea latte for me, every morning on the way to work. Taking turns picking which dessert we'd share when we went out for dinner instead of ordering two. Showering together whenever I slept over even though I hated morning showers. When he cleared his throat and laughed at the same time. When he sniffed his yogurt before eating it no matter how new it was.

But I had to go. You understand why, don't you? He wanted a future, but all my weary fingers could bear to hold onto was a past.

"We have to face our past, Charlie. You know that, don't you?" she says. "I have to travel for a while to do that. I always meant to travel and never did. I married too young. I'd regret it if I didn't go.

"But I forgive myself, and that's why I'm allowing myself to go," she continues. "You can do that, Charlotte, you can start over without forgetting about your past. No one said you have to forget."

I tried, but I couldn't forget the way he looked at me that night. When he started talking about all of the things that he wanted for us. But not the way we girls talk about the things we want sometimes amongst ourselves, mindlessly, dismissively. No, the way he talked was like he was going to do something about it. And soon. The night things got serious all of a sudden.

"I don't want children, okay? Never. I don't want children ever," I said as he walked after me

towards my car. We were the last two people in the
office, so I didn't care if I was yelling.

I made sure that was the last thing either one of
us said, before he could tell me it was alright, and
we didn't have to. It was just something that he
said. He just wants to be with me, he would have
said. He just wants to marry me. We'd be happy
together.

She looks happy, packing her life away.
She looks happy, acting like she's young again.
She looks happy, trying to teach me about life.
And that's what does it. That's really why I
decide that I should stay.

And that's how I left.

Chapter Fifteen: Evie

Mitchell and I pack a backpack each and a recycled grocery bag full of snacks and water bottles for the road. We leave early in the morning. Our stuff tossed into the backseat, the radio running the daily weather report, we are sitting in Mitchell's car and trying to make sense of where we are going.

"He works an hour north of Los Angeles," says Mitchell with one hand on the steering wheel, the other holding up his phone, a screenshot of the clinic website we looked up yesterday on display.

"Okay, so six hours? That's not too bad. I mean, we'll make stops and stuff. And we'll probably stop for lunch. So really, it'll probably be seven hours. That's pretty late. Well, I brought some extra cash if we need a motel or anything. Did you? We'll need gas, too."

"Don't worry."

"I'm not," I say.

"I mean it," he says. "Don't worry."

"Okay."

There's something I haven't told you. A few weeks ago when I was feeling particularly down, I put on my big girl pants and filled out all those forms online—from that organization Mitchell found. The parent hunters.

Not like it matters, all we got in the mail was a page full of kind, discouraging words. The massive amounts of dead ends thrown at them left and right while researching made this case a lost cause. You must really not want to be found.

They did find someone, though. Him. The doctor. Heard he did time because of us.

My stomach feels empty and hollow, like something's growing inside and nothing good. I think some people call it anxiety.

"He has answers," Mitchell said to me last night when I admitted to the whole parent hunters thing, and we did some Internet stalking of our own. We realized we had at least something to justify a road trip across the state. "That makes him a good lead."

His name, George Spolski, was most important. With that we found out where he lives (Ventura, California), where he works (the Ventura Medical Blood Lab), how old he is (fifty-seven, turning fifty-eight in March), and his LinkedIn page, with a semi-large unemployment gap from when he was in jail. But that was so long ago. I'd be surprised if anyone questioned the mysterious lack of work anymore.

We're almost an hour out now and it's beginning to look like rural California outside. Fields of grass beginning to yellow stretch outside our window instead of buildings. Two pigeons fly over a field of orange trees and a third quickens his pace to catch up from behind. Car exhaust and pollen seeps in. A strong springtime breeze tickles my nostrils and my eyes get watery. There is an abandoned-looking barn nearby. I watch as a wooden chair with a broken back struggles and tips over to a gust of wind.

~

A heavenly-looking Spanish style double door and blue and yellow flowerbeds against the building's white exterior make up the Ventura Medical Blood Lab. I feel like we fell into an oil painting. So much stillness. Too much. Too easy. We've even found his designated parking space, after seeing him pull in and out of the same spot, marked reserved, for what must have been his lunch break.

We wait about an hour and a half in the car with a static country music radio station running in the background, and when the doctor pulls out looking exactly like the black and white mug shot we studied half a million times by now, my feet start twitching with energy. It's time to go.

"Excuse me?" I hurry out of the passenger seat towards him. Mitchell's waiting in the car.

"Yes?"

"Hi, I'm Evie Mission. I wanted to speak with you." I pull out and unfold the news clip from my front jean pocket. Headline: State Child Authorities Flag Illegal Third Trimester Abortion. "I think you were there during my birth."

He looks at me as if I were the one in the mug shot. He's caving. No, he's frightened. He's turning into stone.

"You knew my mother? I have questions. That's it. I was wondering if you've heard anything about where she went, after. If you remember anything at all."

"I'm sorry. You got the wrong guy," he says.

I'm not sure what I'm expecting. He's mulling over words, I can tell.

"I can't help you," he tries again.

"But you knew her a little bit," I say.

He disappears behind the automatic doors leading into the clinic. We never go inside. We sit outside, in the car, and wait.

~

That's not to say we just hide behind our car doors and wait for him. We do lots of things. We look up the closest fast-food restaurants and take turns getting takeout from nearly every one of them. We play a lot of tic-tac-toe on an old notepad we find in the glove compartment. Mostly we walk circles around the parking lot.

Every morning, every lunch hour, and every evening on his way home, I try to talk to him. I'm not aggressive, or rude. I don't yell, I don't smile. I just try to talk to him. Mitchell stays back, watches. I think eventually he gets bored, but doesn't have the heart to tell me. We do this for three nights.

Eventually, the man tells me I can't just corner people. "I've been working for over thirty years," he says. "Hundreds of patients come and go. Do you think I remember every single one of them?"

"I think you remember the ones you go to jail for."

But mostly, he just ignores us.

~

Halfway through day four, as he climbs into his car without a word, I decide enough is enough. We did not drag ourselves to the other side of the state for this. The madness must end, one way or another, this is clear to me.

But what is there for me to do? Grab him by the collar, shake him, beg him for something, anything? If any thought had gone into this confrontation, let's be honest, we would have never found ourselves camping out in this medical clinic's parking lot. Mitchell and I would have stayed home.

Doing the same song and dance over and over again and expecting something different to happen is the definition of insanity, I know. Certain that no one will notice aside from me anyhow, I make the only change that I can think of. I begin to raise my voice. Like I do with the kids.

"Excuse me. Sir!" I try to catch up with him.

"What is it exactly that you came here for, miss?"

This stops me. How embarrassing. How embarrassing that not only did I not expect this question, I haven't even really thought of an answer. What am I harassing this man for?

The answer is an apology, I suppose. But an apology won't do much.

Information? *What was she like? Was she scared? Was she angry? With me? Does her voice sound like single raindrops or crashing waves in the nighttime? Did she watch as you carried me away*

from her arms, or did she refuse to hold me at all,
with her chin turned away to the other side of the
pillow and her eyes cast downward? Is her hair
brown and wavy like mine? Is her laugh just like
thunder, in a good way or a bad? Is she real? Is she
still real?

"I guess I just want to know what happened," I
finally say.

The doctor sighs. "I don't know, someone must
have dropped you off at the adoption agency. The
family was waiting for you. They're always by the
phone waiting, with adoption."

"They didn't want me."

It's hard to see outside during the lunch hour
when the sun is at its brightest, but I think he rolls
his eyes. "I'm sorry to hear that," he says.

~

With backaches from too many nights sleeping
in the reclined front seats of Mitchell's car, we
speak to him one last time.

He pulls his car up beside us. His driver's seat
window is rolled down halfway. We stare at each
other.

"Whatever it is you need, you won't find it
here," he says. His longs arms cradle his steering
wheel. In his own tired way, he looks comfortable,
finally. "Don't come back here."

I twist in my seat so that we're making eye
contact. Mitchell is tapping the steering wheel with
his thumb, an unintentional soundtrack of urgency,
a ticking. Talk fast, it seems to be saying to me. Say
anything, anything at all, before he runs away again.

"Can't you at least try to remember her name for me? Just think for a little while and see if you can remember. Please," I say. "I just want a name."

George starts the engine, changes gear into reverse, pulls away. He parks in his usual reserved parking spot.

Chapter Sixteen: Charlotte

Ben knew some things back then.

Like, how I had one serious boyfriend in my life before, from high school. Things didn't end well. My parents both frustrated me and were the most important people in my life. Their opinions were everything. I didn't know what I wanted to do with my life. Staying up all night talking was my favorite intimate activity, and we'd do it all of the time, even when he was tired or one of us had an early meeting the next day.

Here's what Ben didn't know, and still doesn't: I was pregnant once. There was an adoption plan, and then that changed. There was a plan to make it all go away. That changed too.

Deep down he must have known that I couldn't love him right.

With Keith, it was let me throw all of me at you and pray that you won't let me slip between the cracks to my lonesome self again, because that person forgot how to stand on her own two feet. It was getting angry with the man serving me at the coffee shop for being impatient when asking me for my order, because how could he possibly expect me to think about anything else besides our own miserable little breakup for a minute; when my chest felt like the deepest and duskiest of black holes and I couldn't possibly let the world forget it for a moment. It was numbness, in every part of me, aside from the raw, lonely parts.

But with Ben, love was something else. It was not noticing silence when we were together. Smiling while I curled up on the couch, while he bit his fingernails as he concentrated on *The New York Times* crossword. It was taking the time at the store to buy some white roses that I thought would look especially beautiful by his kitchen window. It doesn't matter which one of us bought it. It was sounding dumb when I wondered aloud if sour cream expires but still believing he thought I was smart. People think romance is all flames and passion, but it's not; real romance is completely ordinary.

A night thought I get often is this one, it's a memory. We were searching the suburban streets of San Jose for Christmas lights, the sort of streets that normally stay free of many people but full of lawn ornaments and such as proof that we are all still around and trying our best in a general sort of way. That night was no exception.

Ben and I laced our fingers and lightly swayed our hands as we walked on the part of the street just off the sidewalks, everything around us crisp with dewdrops the way it always is after a winter rain. We just finished dinner at a small Thai restaurant around the corner that gave out banana-flavored toffee with the check.

"Look at us," Ben said and gently pushed his shoulder into mine. "Two wild kids out on the town on a Tuesday night."

He twirled me around once and sat us down on the sidewalk across from the house with the most decorations: a blown up, five-foot tall snow man with a red Santa Claus hat and a green scarf. Christmas lights that changed colors dangled from the roof, bordered the garage door and the second-floor balcony with the French doors. There were hand-painted arrows that trailed the cement walkway up to a sign that said, "Welcome to the North Pole." Fake snow piled up at the front doorstep.

We just sat there, for hours, cuddled under his coat. Hot chocolate in our hands. I knew I could sit that way forever. That scared the shit out of me. I was in love. And he knew absolutely nothing about you.

It's not that I loved Keith more. It's not that he was any better. I just believed in things, back then, expected things like falling in love to be magical, to feel like air. Not the empty kind of air. Not the kind that's slave to the greed of humans. The endlessly massive kind. The kind that opens up and fills you up, too. The kind that spreads like a forest fire and glows just the same, but skips and dances on the tip of the pine trees.

I just couldn't convince myself that this was real, not all the way, the way I did with Keith. Keith got the emotions Ben deserved. Time must be funny that way. It steals things, emotions, before it's even ours to give and receive.

As we sat there together, I slipped my hands into my coat pockets and grinned at the unexpected heat waiting for me there.

"What's this?" I asked and pulled out the handwarmers he must have snuck into my pockets when I wasn't looking.

"You're always so cold, kid," said Ben as he shrugged. "I got tired of hearing you complain about it."

"I told you, nobody uses these in California." I held out one of the handwarmers and giggled.

The doorknob of the Christmas light home jiggled for a split second and then a woman wrapped in a cream-colored, wool sweater walked out by herself towards the green car parked in the driveway. It only took me a moment to recognize the quiet, stomp-like walk as Jenny's, from our finance department at work.

I immediately felt flustered. Ben and I weren't a secret. We weren't telling the person standing behind us in line for the only available coffeemaker on our eighty-person office floor either.

Ben wasn't flustered at all. He lifted his arm from around my waist and gave Jenny a big wave. She looked just as embarrassed as I did as she unlocked her car and waved back.

"Are you okay?" Ben asked me after rewrapping me in his arm.

"Oh, yeah," I responded. "She just doesn't strike me as the Christmas cheer type. Jenny."

"Right. Who knew?" Ben shrugged. "Anyway, have you finished packing for this weekend? What time should I plan to pick you up Saturday morning?"

"Saturday? What's going on Saturday?" I asked while fumbling with the zipper of my coat.

"Earth to Charlotte. The cabin in Tahoe. My family reunion. Remember?" He went on. "You know, we might as well drive down with my parents. Going to the same place. When do you think you'll be ready to go by?"

"Oh that. I think I should stay back," I said. "I told my mom I'd help her with some stuff around the house. And there's work, too."

"What? Charlotte, I've been talking your ear off about this weekend for months. You told me weeks ago that you're coming."

"No, I told you I'd think about it."

"Do you not want to go?" he asked.

"Can we please not make this a big deal? Of course I want to go. But, you know. Anyways, you honestly won't even notice I'm not there, with all your cousins around you, and aunts and uncles, and your dad—"

Ben looked back at Jenny's driveway, though it'd been a while since she left.

"One more question," he said.

I sighed. "Yup?"

"We're not a secret, are we?"

I rolled my eyes and playfully pushed him. "Of course not. It's just the job. It's my first one. And I've been bailing on my parents so much lately, I think they forgot what I look like. What's the rush? I'll go to the next family thing, I promise."

He shrugged. "Alright, fine. But we better not be a secret, kid. Work or not. I've already told everyone all about us, anyway." He winked at me.

My face was still a little warm. I looked down at the handwarmers. I looked at where Jenny had been and her average life, aside from all those damn lawn decorations, and wondered if she had a boyfriend. For whatever reason, it seemed impossible to me. And I went home and cried for people like Jenny because there's nothing sadder than waiting for something that is never going to happen.

~

You could say walking out of a rundown abortion clinic was an out-of-body experience. There are a few things that I remember. I was the last to leave and the outside world was swirling. When walking away, I immediately found myself in the middle of a strong, circling wind. It was 9:23 p.m. and I was feeling terribly alone and afraid that I was slowly breaking. There was drying blood on the seam of my dress, and as hard as I tried to straighten my back and just walk, for the love of God, my legs grew in trembles. Something close to a miracle got me to the nearest bus stop, where I took the three largest steps of my life to climb in through the back door, grip the handrail with whatever bits of energy I had left, and close my eyes.

For the next few weeks, my body felt nothing but empty.

And Keith, well, he was gone; the last I'd seen of him he was in a rush, and he was swearing, and the practitioner was swearing, and Keith wrapped you up awkwardly in the off-white hand towel he always kept in his gym bag and the two of you left me behind.

Three and a half days later we got a call from the police station where you were dropped off. The police station, of all places, as if you were lost. I suppose it didn't take long for the hospital and adoption agency to put their heads together and figure out whose baby you were. My parents told me the next morning that you were taken away to find a family that could care for you.

"What about the Rileys?" I asked.

They made up some excuse to leave the room for a minute. As I filled a coffee mug with some orange juice left on the kitchen counter, I knew there would be an unspoken agreement between the three of us, to carry on through an unbearably hushed few months and our lives would then be, for the most part, back to normal.

What did normal feel like, again?

"God help her," I heard my father whisper to my mother from the hallway, and then break into a muffled sob.

"God help all the little girls," she replied, and I imagined her with dry eyes rubbing his back the way only mothers know how.

~

I watched my parents take care of their own parents so well when I was a kid that I'd forget how once, before I was born, it must have been the other way around. They made it seem simple. Easy. I doubt I would have done it right—the whole parenting thing.

When there was me and you, even for just a little while, it never crossed my mind that I could become childless. That wasn't a fear. I feared being left parentless.

After it all happened, they were my only support system. They took me back in after I ran away. They took me back when I disobeyed, and messed up, and just hated myself and wanted to curl up in a ball and die. My mother made me herbal tea with lemon and honey every morning and my dad served it to me in bed with waffles or scrambled eggs, encouraging me gently to eat up and get out of bed this time. There were lots of *what ifs* floating around in the back of my mind, weighing me down so severely, so heavily.

I spent all of my time wondering, what if God is like the rest of the parents—supposed to be perfect, but just isn't? He overreacts, or gets angry over something that isn't entirely our fault and punishes us. He can be frustrated and make bad decisions, or be selfish, or overreact. He can be tempted and fooled. He can be wrong, sometimes. But he still loves us, and he still tries.

Would He be enough, that way?

When Ben came into my life, normal felt like the worst mistake in the world.

Chapter Seventeen: Evie

We're still here. I can't tell you why. We sit outside the blood lab and wait. Mitchell takes to tapping his right foot and I take to picking at the dried skin around my fingernails until it burns. The weather gets a little warmer, we sleep inside of the car with our feet up on the dashboard and mouths open, we eat from vending machines or at fast food restaurants no more than five miles away. The days get a little longer and the nights a little shorter, we talk a bit and then we don't. We sit and wait.

The practitioner is not so angry anymore, but he tells us to go home again. Go to the adoption agency. Go to a motel, go to a therapist, go anywhere, anywhere but here.

~

We wonder if the Ventura adoption agency can access information from the Bay Area. They can, they tell us, but they can't share anything about a closed adoption.

"I wasn't really adopted," I say. "It was canceled after I was born."

"That doesn't matter." The young woman at the help desk pushes her thick, brown glasses up and cancels the print job on her desktop.

So that's it. All we did for the past six days was sit, and eat cheap food until our stomachs hurt, and hope, and now we will have to go home and forget all about our little adventure on the road. We will have to get back into Mitchell's car that smells of Hot Cheetos and uneasy sleep, and take turns driving up the 101 for the next six hours, and I'll swallow my spit methodically and pretend I'm not carsick so we don't have to stop, and Mitchell will keep asking me how I'm feeling because he always seems to know when I'm lying, and it'll be great. Just great.

"I'm sure you've come across plenty of people trying to trace their biological families down," says Mitchell. "Can't you recommend something for us to try next, something that worked for them? Someplace with answers?"

"I said the exact same thing to all of them that I'm now saying to you," she says. "Anything that happened to them beyond that, I have no idea."

"So, you're telling me they all just threw their hands up and went home?" Mitchell tugs at the hair behind his left ear as he speaks. It is a weird habit of his I see him do a lot lately. He really needs a haircut.

"Maybe. Maybe they found some other resources," the woman at the desk says, pulls the glasses off her face and rolls the brown plastic tip that rested on her ear moments earlier around in her palm. "I hope you find what you're looking for, I really do, but I have to ask you to leave now. There's nothing I can do to help."

~

"*Other resources*," I mock as Mitchell shifts to a lower gear for the downhill ride from the coastline into the open, tan fields that litter the central part of the state. "What does that even mean?"

"Nothing. She was just trying to sound smart," says Mitchell, pulling out a wrinkly looking thing from his back pocket. "Good thing my hand somehow ended up in that stack of papers she tried to toss."

"Mitchell. You didn't."

"I did."

"That's so illegal," I say.

"Impressed?"

"No."

"Ouch. But I just broke a law for you," he says.

"Yeah, and you did a shit job at it," I say. "How did you manage to only get half a page? I can barely read this." I hold up the ripped bottom half of what looks to be a poorly scanned copy of a contract and squint.

"Well, no shit. She ripped it up about a hundred times since she started printing and then remembered she couldn't tell us anything. And I didn't exactly have time for a leisurely read to make sure it was all there."

"Mitchell?"

"Yeah?"

"There are names on here. Two. With signatures."

"What is it? Male and female? Your mom and dad?"

"It could be anyone."

"No. It couldn't." Mitchell narrows his eyes at me. "They have the same contact information so they must have been married, or at least related. See, Mr. and Mrs. Riley." His eyes scan the paper from over my shoulder quickly. We Google their names.

"That area code is in Nevada," says Mitchell.

"I don't know," I say.

"Why not?"

"It can't be right. I was born in San Jose. I think."

We ride silently for a while. "I forgot for a second that I don't know anything anymore," I finally say.

Mitchell gives me a half smile. "Sure you do," is all he says. He slows down at a highway exit with an arrow pointing to a gas station. "So," he starts again. "Do you want Poptarts or pretzels for dinner?"

We ride away from the streets leading to home, away from the browning patches of land and Californian mountain peaks, and somehow deal with the heat.

~

There are Mickey Mouse ears blushing against the darkness of the sky, behind a gate and some happy screams as Mitchell and I sit on the sidewalk outside a souvenir shop in Downtown Disney, the closest to Disneyland either of us has ever been. Mitchell eats his caramel covered apple and I stare at mine, heavy and dangling off a thin plastic stick that I clasp between two of my fingertips, too pretty for me to eat.

"If you could fuck any Disney character, which one would you pick?" asks Mitchell.

"Simba," I say.

"Really?"

"No."

"I'd say Ariel. Definitely," he says.

"Interesting."

"Why?" He asks.

"Guys never pick the redhead. I thought for sure you'd go for Cinderella."

"Nah. She's too dirty for me."

"Hah," I say. "You know the little mermaid died in the original story?" I pick some sprinkles off my caramel covered apple and let them fall over the sidewalk.

"Does she die as a human or a fish?"

"Well, she turns into air for a couple hundred years." I consider if that's really dying. I shrug. "Close enough. Still interested?"

"Is she still a redhead?"

I throw a littered *Lays* bag I find by our feet at him.

"Hey, didn't you used to be a redhead?" Mitchell asks.

"Sure was."

"That's the only time I ever remember you changing your hair color. How come?"

"You don't remember?" I ask.

Mitchell shakes his head.

Just then a crowd comes. A travel group of some sort, it seems. They're all wearing matching red and white striped caps with blue-starred Mickey Mouse ears popping out. Among them, a woman pushing an empty stroller, with two little girls fighting over her free hand. She runs the stroller over my toes as she turns around to scold a little boy for poking a hole through a water bottle and squirting it at people. She says we're in a drought and need to be thankful.

"Then why do we still have to take baths?" asks one of the girls.

"Or brush our teeth?" asks the boy.

"Or wash our hands?" asks the girl again.

"That's different," mumbles the woman. "Besides, all princes and princesses wash their hands before dinner," she says, smiling at the little girl.

I curl and uncurl my toes a few times to get the blood flowing and the pain passing, and wonder if Mitchell is listening.

"I think it's time we head out," Mitchell says to me, to which I agree and think of how no one ever tried to coax me into doing things as a kid just because it was how Disney royals did it. Seems genius. I should try it at work.

~

Maybe I should go back to Orphan Annie red. Little tufts of orange, the hair dye still sticking to the skin of my temple, the weightless, soaking sensation.

For as long as I can remember, I hated my untamable hair, all the waves and curls. Even without the red, I was still a fire alarm. An irresistible target to pull. Carrie was a puller. She loved to call me Annie instead of Evie while I was still a brunette and sing "The Sun will Come Out" during math class. She'd shred construction paper in between her fingers and play games with whoever was sitting next to her, taking turns placing the pieces in my hair one by one until I noticed.

Joining her talent show gig was every ten-year-old girl's dream. She choreographed a slightly different dance routine to some Christina Aguilera song, and won, every year.

I never wanted to dance with her. I thought she was fake and the dance always ridiculous, but I learned rolling your eyes at someone doesn't make all the things you dislike about them disappear.

Anyway, like the most pull-worthy curls, the orphan thing was just too easy. At least for Carrie. If anything, the other kids teased me for the wobbling. But for not having parents? It seemed like a strange reason, even to me. Either way, I preferred the teasing to the sympathy. I thought about it less.

One day, I was walking home when I had a great idea. I'd take away the one thing Carrie cared about most. I'd take her undefeated talent show away from her.

I had just made my way through the neighborhood park I always walked through, taking my time picking up nickels and dimes I found on the sidewalk. Some months I'd collect enough to buy myself hot cocoa from one of the stands near the park benches. It was a fun treat, swinging my feet below the bench as I sipped, listening to the natural rush of cars and people, the distant chirps of baby birds hidden in tree branches, and the gentle swish of falling leaves in autumn.

I was walking extra slow because my jean bottoms were drying out. Earlier I sat on a black piece of construction paper sneakily placed on the seat of my chair with a fresh coat of red paint on it. The teacher yelled at Carrie and called her parents, and offered me a pair of spare gym shorts meant for girls who got their first period during class. I didn't take the shorts, walked just as slow as I always did on my way home. She had taken it too far this time, I remember thinking.

Some movement from the side of my eye stopped me. A studio. People moving around, twirling, leaping. A modest little local dance studio right at the end of the park with large glass windows. That's where I got the idea.

Tap dancing was fun. The pressure shot up my leg at first, especially as I tripped on the sidewalk cracks while trying to shuffle, but it was the sort of pain that seemed worth having—a this-will-make-you-stronger sort of pain.

The dance instructor was a short, young woman that always looked warm and smiled, and kindly never said a word when she'd see me outside. Sometimes she'd even leave those miniature water bottles on the bench outside the studio for me before class.

I penciled my name in on the lined paper hanging next to the drinking fountain at school for talent show auditions. Then I went to the Walmart across the street, bought a 99-cent bag of pretzels and orange hair dye, and skipped all the way home.

I haven't seen Carrie for years. I hear she's a life coach now.

I still have the little first place ribbon on my keychain from my Annie-inspired tap number in the talent show. Silly, I know, but I'm still proud of making it as the mold Carrie thought I could never fit.

But girl who goes on an impossible journey to find her long lost mother? A moving reunion? That's the real mold I just can't seem to fit.

~

When looking down over the highway at the passing vehicles during nighttime, the only thing we can see is light. We're high up in the mountains now. She squiggles and pulses and glows, I love being blinded in the nightfall by man-made lights. The light is a she, I know, and I know that she is mine. She makes the world seem smaller and somehow manageable. I think of all the people inside the cars around us, so many people I can't see but so close to where I am, and I know it is so.

She is right. The world must be small and somehow manageable.

~

It hasn't rained in months.

The gutters and porches fill up with dried leaves, and pale weeds litter the side streets as we enter Nevada. We drive all night, through an odd heat that falls down on us like bullets and wind that draws us backwards and upwards. Mitchell's small but mighty Nissan manages to climb up a mountain and when we stop in front of a woodsy-looking house that is wide, looming, and beautiful, we just sit for a while. The radio says we're heading into wildfire territory.

Chapter Eighteen: Charlotte

Since coming home, I find that San Jose is one of those cities that has managed to out Silicon Valley itself. From all the people flocking in, to the new skyscrapers going up, it has gone through a complete transformation. It has reinvented itself.

We drive for a few minutes up the 101 to get to downtown. Shuttles of employees behind tinted windows clog up the highway. Start-ups and over-priced coffee shops with crowded Wi-Fi networks and soft rock playing seem to dominate every corner. The Apple store on the busy corner and the Lululemon next door are the two hot spots. We must squeeze by loitering groups out on the sidewalk, and my mother hates touching strangers. Well, at least she used to hate it.

When we step inside the heated room with the college banners and the shed-like walls, I feel like we've made it to another planet somehow. A hole in the wall sort of place—I can't even figure out the official name of this bar. The logo is wordless with a useless picture of a martini glass on it. It's on one of the side streets that extends from the busyness of the normal shops and restaurants (with real logos).

175

My mother and I are very clearly out of place, and not just because we are the two oldest people here. She's in flare jeans and a mocha knit sweater, I'm in leggings and a thick cardigan. We either need to tear our clothes up a little or grow beards.

This was how it all began: I found her sitting in our dining room, bursting with energy as she scribbled a bunch of words down on a napkin in red ink. She said she was working on her bucket list, and that I was going to help her with it.

"A *bucket list*? Mother, you are not dying."

"Oh, that's not what those are about!"

"Oh, really? What are bucket lists for, then?"

"Quite the opposite. Living? Making the most of what you've been given? Doing the things you've always wanted to do, but never had a chance to?" She used the feathered pen she was holding to bonk me on the head as she spoke.

Task one of the bucket list was on tonight's agenda for mother and daughter.

"Why are we here, again?" I ask, trying to push past a group of enormously tall guys all wearing flannel shirts and large glasses too big for their faces. I'm trying to get to the bar for no specific reason. I'm not in the mood to drink. Pushing just seems to be the acceptable thing to do here when you first walk in.

"It's karaoke night," Mother says. "It's the easiest item on my list," she adds.

The band sets up in the corner of the cozy-sized room and the bartender places two napkins in front of us. My mother orders a mojito and I order a ginger ale with a lemon slice.

"Hope there's a good crowd tonight," my mother says.

"There will be," the bartender says. The clock behind him reads 9:38. "You've got time."

"So," I say as I wipe my hand on the back of my thighs. There's a puddle of vodka on the bar top. "What are you planning on singing?"

At this, she perks up. She's been practicing the same song now for a while, something by Michelle Branch. Since when does she listen to Michelle Branch? Mom tells me how happy she is to finally find a local place where she can perform, something fun and not "too serious."

I remember her singing under her breath sometimes when driving, or washing the dishes, or whatever, but she sang her songs so subtly and to herself that trying to listen in felt like intruding.

My mother likes reasons. Reasons for everything. So did my dad. They grew up that way. Dad was raised in Utah by an ex-military priest and Mom in way up north California, where she says the rain eventually washed the tomboy out of her. When she hit eleven years old and became a homebody, her mother and two older sisters took an interest in her and taught her to apply blush and lip liner. Then Stella, the oldest of the three girls, dodged a deer on the highway one late night. The deer survived, Stella didn't. After that, Mom vowed to get away as soon as she became a grown up and never go back to visit her ghosts.

Mom and Dad met in college and fell in love in history class. They were pronounced man and wife under the oak tree outside of Dad's Utah home that's been here longer than any of us, her age a beautiful secret between herself and the nearby bushes that danced behind the dinner guests during the chillier part of the reception.

She never really made any sense, my mother. She'd nod along with my father on all reason and logic, but on the other hand, she was always superstitious. We weren't allowed to open up umbrellas indoors. She'd read our monthly horoscopes at the first of every month. She knocked on wood all of the time. She'd be the ground beneath my feet, then get back to worry and shenanigans and chaos. That's why when the only reason I get out of her is, "I don't know. Because it's fun?" I must ask again.

"But why?" I start. "Why do we have to be *here*? It's so—"

"Unlike us?" She tries to hide a smirk.

The band starts playing—show time. A piece of binder paper is passed around among the growing crowd inside of the bar. My mother places her name on the sign-up sheet; she's fourth on the list.

"I still have a bit more packing to do, of course. But I hope we'll be able to tackle two or three items from the list per week," she says. Then she adds in perky voice, "Then maybe you could add some of your own bucket list items."

I stab the seeds in my lemon slice with my straw and stare at her.

"Or not. Whatever you decide," she says.

We hold each other's hands as we get up from the bar stools and walk in zigzags towards the front of the stage. A sharp melody from the saxophone pours into the next song and a group of head bobbing people form. A few brave souls start to dance. The dim lights dip even lower as the speakers settle in, strobe lights swirling on the ceiling and on the Spanish tiled floor, the air shrinking and sucking us all in close. I stay near my mother. She's tapping her foot with arms crossed across her torso and looking at the band.

The first karaoke act is a big group of friends, and no one pays attention as they laugh more than they sing. Then there's a Rascal Flatt's song, a man whose southern twang is actually quite impressive, and I remember that most of the people in this room are transplants. What does he think of us—self-obsessed, robotic, workaholic, lost-in-ourselves—which of these Silicon Valley stereotypes are really true? Though it's not like I can claim any of these, not any longer. Who knows why I've fallen into a *one-of-them* mindset here, the place I haven't lived, or even visited, for years.

I ask my mom if she's nervous and she tells me that she knows it's silly, but she's been waiting for this for so long, she can't tell if its nervousness, or excitement, or something else.

"Really?" I ask. "I didn't know singing actually meant that much to you. How come you never sang in the church choir, or anything like that?"

"Oh, there was always something, you know," she says. She twirls a hair gently around her index finger and straightens her back so surely, she's beginning to convince the both of us that she really belongs here. I start pulling at my own sleeves. "You know, *something*. Another family reunion or upcoming event to plan for, some more paperwork to push around, another new student to work with." Before she retired, my mother was a speech therapist at the local elementary school. She shrugs. "And that's how the old story goes."

Her name is called. Mother walks around the crowd and takes the five little steps on the side of the stage up instead of taking one giant lunge onto center-stage. She trots over to the band, stage-right, whispers her song into the guitarist's ear, and remains quiet, clutching the propped-up mic without adjusting it.

Now she looks nervous. I want to make up an excuse to drag her away and keep her from this place forever, somewhere warm, and safe, and full of smiles and fusses over each other, or anything she wants.

And so, your girl is gone, or is it just a rumor? She begins, her singing voice exactly how I expect it to be.

She knew it must be wrong, 'cause she'd been crying, crying far too long. I know the way she feels, although I never knew her. While you're out having fun...

She starts shaking her hips from side to side, but a small shake, so it's not too much and even kind of cute.

But if you happen to call, and tell me it wasn't my fault, how all of this time you were wrong, would I even pick up the phone?

Swaying, twirling my arms around, I begin a dance of my own. I bob in a sea of moving bodies. Dancing alone and together in a single pulse, lip-syncing the words I hardly know, a giggle bubbling up behind my teeth. Now I'm spinning in circles, round and round myself till I feel I am going to burst to my mother's sweet, honey-drenched singing voice.

~

We knit and donate fifty scarves to the homeless. It probably will not matter much to anyone besides ourselves that they are scarves made from hand—four very sore hands—but to us, hitting fifty was exciting enough to finish the half bottle of cabernet blanc in the fridge left over from mother's going away party. This bucket list item, I'll admit, was a good one.

The next one is ridiculous.

"I've always wondered what it'd be like, ever since the *Little House on the Prairie* series. Do you remember watching those together on PBS every Thursday afternoon right after school? Remember? Oh, you were too young."

"I remember. And Mom, this wasn't featured in any of those episodes."

She shoos my memories away with her free hand, the other on the computer mouse, still scrolling down the local goat farm website. Though neither of us managed to hear of this place until good ol' Google ads suggested it about a week into the bucket list challenge, the goat farm is about forty-five minutes away. It's right off the coastal 1 highway, and its site tours are booked full for the next three and a half weeks.

"No need for a tour," my mother says. "I've emailed the owner of the place and she said she's more than willing to show us the ropes. Her husband is back east for the next two weeks and she could use the extra hands."

Roxana Ellen tells my mother that if she doesn't want to miss the kidding, we'll either have to stay on the farm for a few days or be on call for a quick drive over, fifteen- or twenty-minutes tops. Since we'd have to rent a place to stay to make it in time anyway, we opt for staying in Roxana Ellen's guesthouse.

The place certainly looks like a farm. Its mistress, Roxana Ellen, certainly does not look like a farmer. Mother wears cowgirl boots and a bright red flannel shirt tied up in a knot in the front.

Roxana Ellen smiles a lot and is real bossy, dragging the two of us by the arm to where we should be standing, and grabbing the stirring bowl from our hands to make sure the vitamin supplements are in there good for the soon-to-be mother goats, and talking eighty miles an hour in a neutral tone.

Roxana Ellen puts me to work sweeping the barn out of hay "bedding," undressing the tiled floor because of the warming months. This space will be a bonding stall soon for the new baby goats. The barn is a wide space and I wonder how many goats live here currently.

Thirteen goats, Roxana Ellen tells me. She seems very proud about it and not worried by the unlucky number.

Roxanna Ellen's son stares at me while I take a break. I'm leaning against a wooden broom while my mother spends some time with the friendliest of the goats, the ones that let her pet their thick fur. The young boy doesn't leave his place by the door until his sister calls for him to come play some video game with her. He has perfectly round, chipmunk cheeks and a bowl cut.

Roxana Ellen has three kids. Besides the little one, who is just a few months old, they all do what they can to help the farm.

Who knew farmgirling was such hard work? My wrists are already sore and flyaway hairs keep sticking to my forehead.

The next day, Roxana Ellen's boy sets up a tin bowl underneath a faucet like the one at public beaches for rinsing feet. He whines at his mother when she tries to carry it away herself. Instead, he grips both ends himself and waddles over to the roped off section of the barn with about half the water still inside the bowl. The other half, spilling and gathering on the floor. All the while Roxana

Ellen trails behind him closely without saying a word, something he seems okay with.

My mother and I each grab a handle of a plastic tub full of the hay I swept away earlier and march it outside in perfect rhythm. We've just barely finished setting up and I can already hear the television coming from inside Roxana Ellen's home, the front door wide open.

We don't eat with Roxana Ellen and her children. We sit outside on her doorstep while Roxana Ellen nurses her baby girl inside and wait for the beet salad and baked chicken she promised to bring out to us once it's ready.

We've already began to memorize the goats' names.

"The one with the freckles is Betty," Mom says, and I know exactly who she is talking about. The most senior female in the pack, pure white fur with orange freckles falling down her baggy chin. We point out the rest. Ted is the tallest, broad shouldered one. Cinnamon, the pusher. Jay, the mutt of the pack. Cinnamon likes to dip her head in a charge and chase Jay away from the water tap just for fun.

One gray goat with two brown dots on his hind leg trots by us, the yellowing layers of pulled grass denting softly beneath his feet. The sunset is beginning to slow these days and I have no indication of what time it is without looking at my phone, aside from my growling stomach slowly churning to a soft murmur.

"Dinner is served," Roxana Ellen says as she places a stack of paper napkins and a saltshaker on the floor next to where we sit. "And an extra piece of garlic bread for you," she says as she places the kiss of the bread on my plate.

"Thanks," I say with a close-mouthed smile and glance down at my plate. "This is all great. Thank you."

She dismisses herself back to her children, who have just recently discovered the volume button on the TV remote.

Roxana Ellen is trying to be extra nice to me. She can tell she offended me when she asked me what I do for a living and didn't understand my answer when I said I wasn't sure what's next for me or how long I was staying in California for yet. Most people let it go. Roxana Ellen is the type of woman who keeps going.

"You don't have to get defensive with her, you know," Mom says, dipping a piece of garlic bread into the beet juice collecting at the bottom of the slightly tilted plate resting in her lap.

"Not defensive, Mom."

We eat. She is looking at me, though, in a way that makes me wonder what she believes I'm going through. What she thinks that I am thinking right now.

Maybe the fact that I'm thirty-six years old, for God's sake, and am eating a meal perhaps one step above dino nuggets in the hierarchy of age-defining foods from a plastic plate with Minnie Mouse's face on it.

She thinks herself a mind reader, my mother. The biggest problem with mind reading is that it generally turns into a lecture.

"Just turn things around, Charlotte, just do it," Mom begins. "Think of all the beauty, and the unbelievable fortune that can come only from the choices that you make, the choices years from now another you will make. How every inch of life up until this point is the DNA of you. So I guess what I'm saying is, as long as you accept the person you are at this very moment and make the promise to love that person in all of your future days. If you can make that promise wholeheartedly you have nothing to fear, nothing to regret. There is nothing regrettable about you."

I just stare at her, mouth full of chicken. I want to say something snarky, something sharp, but the guilt swelling in my stomach stops me. Sometimes I wonder if the guilt that always follows spending time with my parents was part of the reason that I ran so many years ago, when the three of us lived together still and we pretended you were not something entirely different to feel guilty about.

"Mom," I say, lightly, gently, so as not to be confused for angry or annoyed, the way daughters are sometimes with their mothers. "I'm okay. Truly, I am. I like my life. I'm healthy, I'm able to support myself, all the things I need to do well have been given to me. What do I have to complain about? I'm fine." And then because I feel like there's still a hole in our heart-to-heart, I add, "I only really stayed for so long to help you, like you asked me to. Remember? Otherwise, I'd be off to my next gig."

Not visiting home all of this time was a lot easier than it sounds. I managed to dodge a few Christmases and a number of Easter weekends in the beginning, claiming holiday season was tough for us in the travel industry, which is not a lie. Eventually we stopped discussing it. Eventually we grew apart.

"I'll be fine. You'll be fine. We'll all be fine at the end of things," My mother says as she wipes her lips with a paper napkin, places her finished plate on the step below her and then signifies a finished meal and final thought by folding her hands in her lap. "If it's not fine, it's not the end," she adds.

We then talk about the goats again, her upcoming travels, and whether or not she should draft up another bucket list for the time she'll spend overseas. I worry about her trying to do too much at once. She tells me there's no such thing as too much at her age. Here I am ironically fearing how old I myself am getting with so little to show for it. My aging mother is a rock.

~

My mother broke every plate in the house that day. "New silverware," she repeated a few times under gasps and squeaks. She was out of breath from all the walking and swinging, back and forth. "Buy it all new." She said we needed a new beginning.

Crack. Shriek. Crunch.

"Not even a teacup. Don't leave even a teacup in sight." She sipped cold, black coffee out of a paper cup. I obeyed, and considered if she was perhaps losing her mind.

The evening news hummed behind us in the next room, a low and steady comfort. The screen showed four cop cars chasing after O.J. Simpson up the Interstate Highway south of Los Angeles. Voices buzzed just loud enough for us to know something major and important was happening, soft enough for us not to understand.

Dad left. Three days ago. But Mom lost it long before.

I first knew it when I looked at her one morning on my way out the door. I was still going to the community college back then. It was early on a Thursday morning, nearly 6:30 a.m., and I wanted to squeeze in a game of tennis on campus before my intro to ethics class. Folding into herself at the kitchen table, huddled in one corner, my father on the farthest opposite corner reading last Sunday's paper. I knew it. Precious fingertips. Frizz and shivers. She was breaking, in a slow, petrifying sort of way. A way I knew no one could help, not him, not I. And yet it would only take one minute for him to do something, anything. He wouldn't. He could reach out and simply not let her droop away. *Don't droop over, don't feel*, I wanted to scream out to her. But I didn't.

They hardly spoke anymore, and when they did it was bitter and sometimes cruel. It was to scold each other for not paying the electricity bill yet or for leaving the kitchen window open for too long, letting the summer heat seep in. It was to stare at each other in the silent way of letting each other know they did something wrong. It was to sigh, or make an eye roll seen, or complain about some habit they probably have been doing for years.

I figured this was all inevitable, because aren't our parents always the exact reference point of the way things should be? Bickering sometimes, getting on each other's nerves the way families can. It was normal.

The plate thing, however, was weird. Even for her.

How dare we love each other, I thought while watching them closely sometimes. *How dare we let each other believe we will save one another when the charm melts away and we are finally left alone to face a vulnerable, careless little thing that is only ours to cherish and to hold.* The thought scared me so much I vowed to never question something as holy as marriage again. The answers I'd get would be too much to accept.

Guilt was there too, of course. I knew everything was connected somehow. You, me, them, mostly me.

I knew he couldn't look at me anymore. His baby girl long gone to the sinful side.

I liked to believe he couldn't help thinking those things about me. I liked to think he left because he knew, deep down, he needed to fix the way things were at home, and yet he wasn't sure how. With the fear of doing the wrong thing so deeply engrained in his mind—was it his own father who told him he'd never be good and pure enough? Was it a line he read late at night as a teenager, somewhere in the history books built on our ancestor's wisdom, somewhere while searching for a clue about life? Whatever it was, something whispered in his ear again and again as he grew from a boy needing guidance to a man.

I worried his leaving was the last straw. I worried my mother wouldn't be able to take it. All I felt was worry. Then one day I came home and he was sitting at the dining room table, same as always, yesterday morning's newspaper in hand. He glanced up momentarily, winked at me, returned to his reading. My mother stirred something smelling of tomato sauce and faint hints of garlic cooking on the stovetop with a pleasant-enough look on her face.

It was so puzzling. He left, he gave up on us, yet here he was. They both let it all be. I never did like letting things work out on their own. I never did like letting it be. We never talked about it again.

My aging mother is a rock.

Chapter Nineteen: Evie

When Mrs. Riley opens her door at precisely 9:51 p.m. while the night flames begin rolling down the Nevada hills, she thinks the two kids on her doorstep are two misfits looking for shelter. Their shifting eyes, dressed in hoodies and jeans faded around the knees. Her husband puts on the kettle, knowing that she is never wrong about these sorts of things.

Still standing there, the kids tell her their names as if she has been expecting them. They say they have some questions for her.

No one is watching the distant treetops blazing from branch to branch any longer. They are set off during close huddles when the wind pulls each and every twig on the stump in close. Mrs. Riley puts down the two jugs of drinking water she was just carrying and steps just a smidge to the left, inviting the two strangers in for no reason other than there isn't a lot of time, and there is so much more to do in preparation for the fire. She can't stand the air during wildfires, and closes the door behind her as quickly as possible.

She brushes a handful of slightly graying brown hairs out of her face and arranges most of a family pack of Oreos on a plate, not the white ceramic one, but the plastic plate with the pale floral design, and sets two cranberry-colored mugs on the kitchen counter.

"Are these friends of Matty's?" Mr. Riley asks his wife.

"I thought so," she whispers back. Two seconds pass and she adds, "But maybe I was wrong. I don't think they are from around here."

Mr. Riley is a man who likes familiar things. He begins his days in the same fashion every morning, with a whole wheat piece of toast coated with two scoops of peach jam and a medium sized coffee with milk, no sugar, poured from the Riley's Keurig. The high whistle it makes as it brews reminds him that he hasn't bought the new air pump yet from the online coffee machine shop he bookmarked two days ago. Mr. Riley will then usually read either the Financial Times or the Huffington Post from his MacBook, or perhaps discuss the state of the most current lab project from his job at a biotechnology company, or which neighbors are rumored to be moving away but never do. He has these talks with his wife during the three or four mornings a week that the two wake at the same time. His son is not to be bothered in the mornings.

After the chores and preparatory chaos of wildfire season and there is nothing left to do but wait for evacuation orders that usually never come,

Mr. Riley likes to pull out his old leather album. The album once belonged only to the solitary confinement of his Grandfather Andrew's glass display case. There, the album was always propped up at a diagonal to suggest something worthy is inside. And indeed, inside is Grandfather Andrew's precious map collection—the Americas with golden trimming, the streets of Paris in sepia colors, a sketch of Pangea—which belonged to the grandfather before him and so forth.

Mr. Riley doesn't keep the old leather album in nearly such a proper place now. He thinks of it in its current respective spot, wedged between old tax files and his high school diploma in his home office where anyone can find it and open it if they'd like. He enjoys the chance to make the collection his own and often thinks of which map should be his first to add. Mr. Riley was never one for travel, but he always knew how to appreciate a nicely laid out map.

He shifts from one foot to the other now, knowing this is one of the first wildfires he may not have a chance to spend flipping through the old leather album. This has been his ritual since the Riley's moved to Nevada from California.

Mrs. Riley, on the contrary, travels within the walls of the home she worked hard to fill with comfort since they bought it in 1997. She's constantly moving something—her hands, her feet, the couch pillows to lean against the armrest correctly after they slip yet again from their place on the leather couch. When she feels, she does so strongly, with a sort of femininity you're not afraid to touch or break. She likes to listen to the radio just to hear the voices of the radio hosts. She has a to-do list but doesn't like to run through the tasks in order.

I like to watch these two together. They seem to be silently speaking to each other, even with their backs turned; I wonder what they are saying.

Mrs. Riley checks her phone and says, "Looks like it's going to be a big one. We'll keep an eye on evacuation orders. Air's going to be terrible. Better stay indoors until tomorrow late morning, maybe afternoon. Do you two have a place to stay?"

I have no idea what she's talking about.

"The fire is beginning to spread," she says. When neither of us reply she shuffles towards the door again quickly. She doesn't look back as she folds a dish towel with one hand and expects us to follow her. "Whatever it is you're selling, we're not interested. Or if it's a charity you two have going, we'll donate. Not to be rude, but we really do need to be quick so we can get going here."

The Mr. and Mrs. both sigh at our blank faces and she says, "Well, you haven't the time to go anywhere else at this point. You can stay with us until it's safe."

Mr. Riley announces that the water is almost boiled, and the kettle gives a ding just as he finishes his sentence. Mrs. Riley is opening up drawers, looking for the facemasks they have stashed away to help with the smoke.

A boy who looks to be around sixteen or seventeen walks into the kitchen.

"Who is that?" Mitchell asks me, looking irritated.

"I have no idea," I say.

"Matty," says Mr. Riley. "We have guests."

"I can't find my headphones, Mom."

"They're right there coming out of your pocket," she says after turning towards him for a moment and then back to the hot cocoa mix that she is scooping into the laid-out mugs.

"No, these are just the earbuds that came with the phone. I mean my green Monster ones."

When it becomes obvious Mrs. Riley doesn't have an answer and isn't about to go searching for one, Matty gives Mitchell and I a nod and swings his feet around the loveseat in the corner.

"Matty, can you get the wool blankets from the trunk, please, baby?" his mother asks. He taps his phone and I hear the dubstep get louder from his little earbuds.

"A wildfire?" says Mitchell. "Shouldn't we leave?"

"To where? There's no time for that, son," says Mr. Riley.

He hands Mitchell two of the facemasks, still warm from the air escaping the dishwasher near where they just rested and Mrs. Riley hands me the two mugs of hot chocolate and I understand that we'd better hurry.

They shut the doors, they lock the windows, they close the vents and the fireplace screen. They remove the curtains. Mr. Riley gets the blanket from the car and takes a moment to reverse out of the garage and face the nose of the Volkswagen towards the street. Mrs. Riley rounds all of us up and we pair off to pull the outdoor patio chairs through the sliding-glass doors and into the center of the living room in a cluster of couches, cushions, upside down coffee tables and rolled up rugs. It looks like a terribly made fort.

Next, Mrs. Riley asks us kids to get the dry foods from the garage. She pulls out a recyclable grocery bag from a kitchen drawer, folds it up, hands it to her son, telling him not to forget the extra water bottles, the medication for his itchy skin in case we'd have to leave, and to pick out a variety of cereal bars, not just the strawberry ones at the top of the box but the apple ones, too, that Dad likes. She unclasps a bracelet from around her left wrist, places it in her pocket, rolls up her sleeves and nods her head once at Mitchell and me as she excuses herself.

~

Their garage is not really a garage. It's carpeted and lined with the wooden insides of a modern bookcase, several shelves floating by their lonesome without a border or any sort of connection from one to the next. On it are novels, empty picture frames, a baseball glove, and an empty *Trouble* game box. There's a brown leather loveseat against the wall and an army print bean bag chair to its right. There's a vent, perhaps a heater, although the place has the cold quality of a fairly neglected room.

The replacement child has a dimple splitting his chin into two, a butt-chin that makes him look one hundred percent dumbass. He props his foot against the closed garage door, lights a joint pulled from his back pocket and passes it. Mitchell takes the first hit, then me.

No one talks and I curl up on the bean bag chair and watch as the replacement child grabs two handfuls of cereal bars and throws it into Mrs. Riley's cotton bag, which Mitchell has already shaken out and placed an eight-pack of juice boxes inside of.

I want to know everything. But he knows nothing. He looks at me funny when I ask too many questions. *How old are you? Did you wish you had siblings when you were growing up? Did your parents? Were you happy together? Did you have family movie nights, and go on road trips, and make each other dinner and handmade greeting cards on your birthdays?*

We talk about California for a little bit, and then we talk about Netflix shows. The replacement child tells us that yes, he is adopted, and he rolls his eyes when I tell him that he's lucky. Kicking off his sneakers, he takes another puff and offers it to Mitchell again.

~

The replacement child is raging. His feet rub up against the carpet floor; he is pacing between clouds of smoke, causing the sort of uncomfortable heat that sometimes spreads like a midnight storm over a quiet mountainside town. His fingertips are blazing, ripping the wrappers off the apple cereal bars and letting them crumble to the ground. He is fumes and embers. He says it is way too fucking hot in here. He is one of those people who burns everything he touches and I'm so tired of it.

"It's so fucking hot," the replacement child says again. He is staring at me and I hate it.

Mitchell is laughing about something, an uncontrollable, enormous sort of laugh.

"What the fuck was in that?" I ask, staring wide-eyed at the replacement child.

He ignores me. "How'd you guys get to this shithole anyway? You're not from here, I can tell." Turning his head, it's clear he doesn't really expect an answer.

"We're on an adventure," says Mitchell.

"An adventure?"

"Yeah, adventure. Don't you ever go on adventures?" Mitchell asks, his dimples accented, thicker than usual.

"Yeah, right," says the replacement child. "My parents don't even let me borrow the car. I guess you're lucky you're not an only child."

"I'm not really her brother," says Mitchell.

"It's too hot in here."

After climbing on top of the loveseat, the replacement child holds his lighter to the fire alarm and the water starts trickling down on us. I watch his mother's cotton grocery bag dampen from a cream color to a darker shade. The apple cereal bars

are all ruined, wet, the outer crumbs shedding off
the fruit spread into a pile on the ground, the
strawberry cereal bars still wrapped and untouched.

Before I know it, I'm boiling, too. Something
inside of me tenses so far back, it grazes my
muscles. My imperfect muscles. It tells me that I'll
feel better once I release some of the storm inside of
me. *Get up,* it whispers. *Get up now, Evie.*

When I punch him, I am breathless. I try
punching him straight in the mouth, but I'm not
very good at it. So I slap him, hard, across the face.
So hard that it makes a clapping sound and the skin
of my palm stings. I try to slap him again, but he
catches my wrist and tries to spin me around into a
chokehold while I bite at his hands.

Mitchell is swearing as he tears me away from
the replacement child and carries me to the other
side of the room. I shake him off, grab a hold of the
bag with the food we managed to pack, regain my
balance. I walk inside the house with that cotton bag
bundled up and safe against my chest.

~

Could we really have bad blood coursing
through our bodies? Is it genetics we're supposed to
blame, or conditions so outside of our control we
only venture there by chance? I am not like Hannah.
I am not considerate or simple. I do not keep
anything in my life as together as Mitchell does.

All I know is that I was perfectly fine living a
life without asking too many questions before you
came along. The real you, in between the lines of a
medical bill.

Chapter Twenty: Charlotte

During mornings on the farm, I quickly learn, you are guaranteed to be sticky with sweat. By the afternoons, you are to be dripping wet with it.

It's past noon and I'm exhausted, still lugging around a half-eaten Eggo waffle because I haven't had a moment of rest since I woke up from a hot and cramped night of sleep, my mother on the couch and me on the floor in a sleeping bag made for children. Turns out the guesthouse is the living room.

Roxana Ellen promised us the full kidding experience this morning. It's an important day for the soon-to-be mother goats. Their pubes are to be cut.

That's right, their downstairs need to be trimmed. And my mother and I are the stupid volunteers who get to do it.

The nursing process is easier this way and much simpler in terms of cleaning up the blood afterwards, I am told. It doesn't stick as much to the tail hairs when the pubic hairs are cut short.

My mother finds an outlet beneath a wooden table around the barn shed and gets going with the electric trimmer with no complaints. Roxana Ellen grabs a small trash can to prop in between her legs and begins clipping her own fingernails.

"What?" She asks when she catches my stare. "Just in case I need to get in there after a stubborn kid," she says and wiggles her fingertips at me.

"Does that happen often?" I ask.

"Not really. In the ideal situation, the farmer is like wallpaper. The last thing we want to do is become the backseat drivers. Let nature take its course, but be prepared to help if needed, and it generally works out."

She tells us about how she plans to sell any of the male kids. There's an online marketplace for it. She already has an alpha male on the farm, as she calls him, a six-year-old named Cocoa. "He gets the job done," she tells us.

I pinch a bit of hair from a white goat's behind and start cutting.

~

The white goat is in the corner where we pushed aside some extra hay. She is pacing, pawing at the hay every once in a while, and breathing heavy.

I turn to call for help, but Roxana Ellen is already there, like an overprotective mother. Which surprises me, frankly, given her previous talk about stepping back and letting the birthing process just be.

"She's in labor," my mother says to no one specific. She comes up behind Roxana Ellen and they escort each other to crouch by the goat's side.

The goat stops pacing within the next five minutes. Standing still, she looks calmer. I stare at her face—mostly to avoid the bloody scene from her other end that both Roxana Ellen and Mom seem so readily available and eager to assist in, if needed. I see the goat mother's discomfort written clearly in the light blue of her eyes. We wait.

There's some more heavy breathing. The stiffening and straightening of her tail, then the final crowning. She has two new baby boys. The first born goes straight to the pen, a large, kicking kid with white fur like his mothers.

The second, however, is hardly kicking. He's almost half the size of his brother. He has one dark gray ear, one brown, and he's struggling to blink his eyes wide open. My mother hands Roxana Ellen the small shot glass she points to silently, which she then fills with iodine and applies to the umbilical cord stub. Then she pulls out a plastic bottle of something that looks like yogurt.

"What is that?" I ask.

"A vitamin E boost," Roxana Ellen replies. "To help him get stronger."

"Is he going to be okay?" Mom asks.

"I don't know," Roxana Ellen says with a very light shrug. "I hope so."

She holds him in her palm, up towards his mother who is leaning against the wall, ready to go in nursing position. He eats, slower and clearly with much less energy than his bigger brother, but still, he eats. When he's done nursing, he makes a weird sound that sounds a lot like the evil laugh villains make in cartoons. Weird quirks start early for goats, apparently. We all laugh.

The three of us women leave the new family in the bonding pen we created, leaving the newborns to marvel at their new home, and for the mother goat and the people who helped build it to marvel right back.

~

We play with the goats for a while the next evening, spreading our feet out on the ground beside them as we pet their backs and feed them hay out of our hands. Our unspoken favorite, the runt of the pack, is now healthy enough to stand and wobble about the barn next to his twin brother.

At one point, I notice my mother slipped out without our noticing, not surprising with these little beasts occupying all of our attention. I find her standing outside of Roxana Ellen's home, looking up at the summer sky which is still brushed with daylight and freckled with night stars appearing where clouds might have been. She looks accomplished.

"So," I say, taking my place beside her. "What's next on the list?"

"I think it's time for us to go home now," she says.

"Can I ask you something?"

"Go ahead," Mom says.

"Why goats?"

She blinks a few times, then replies, "Why not?"

She pulled our bags out from Roxana Ellen's living room already. They now wait at her feet. We both give Roxana Ellen a quick hug. The car keys jangle from my mother's hips where they rest clipped to her jeans.

Just as quickly and as quietly as we first entered this little farm on the Pacific, we part ways with the land. I slip off my flats while sitting in the passenger seat, Mom fans herself with a folded up old grocery list behind the steering wheel, and we reverse out of Roxana Ellen's driveway towards the 17. Back to where we came from, a baby goat with one dark gray ear, one brown, cackling like a hyena behind us.

~

There's a happiness to returning to the same street signs you've seen every day since childhood. Hometowns are important. Hometowns remind us of the smallest, and strongest, comforts in our day-to-day lives. I keep telling myself this. We're back to days filled with logistics, cardboard boxes and suitcases flooding the floor.

Mother is leaving in just a few weeks. What am I to do once she is gone?

I could stay. But what is the point to that?

On the backside of a furniture store sale flyer tucked away in a desk drawer I've been tasked with clearing out, I scribble down a title, "Charlotte's Bucket List." Underlining it twice, I begin to think. *What do I want, what do I want?*

Research some do-it-yourself craft projects. Buy new living room furniture for my mom. Learn how to cut my own bangs. Learn how to ride a motorcycle. Buy the most expensive thing on the menu, just because, just once.

The list grows with whatever the hell I think most people add to these sorts of lists. Skydive, though I don't care too much for heights. Go for a multi-day hike, though I don't care for blistering from uncomfortable boots.

I write until my pen runs out of ink. When I look for another in the other drawers of the desk, I find my old handwarmers, instead. From Ben.

What am I doing?

I rip the list down the middle three times and crumple it up as fast as I can. Riding a motorcycle. Cutting my own bangs. *What am I, eleven years old?*

"I'd say we did good for today." My mother's voice escapes from the big box in the hallway she's crawled into. She's putting the last of her summer dresses inside before taping it up. "All we need to do now is the rest of your bedroom, and the study, and then that's the last of it."

"Great."

"And done a few days earlier than expected. The agent will be pleased. I can't believe another family will be living here." She shakes her head.

"Right," I answer.

"Are you even listening to a word I'm saying?" She inspects the few boxes around the desk I haven't managed to fill. Rolling her eyes, she looks at the desk I'm still sitting at, its surface still swarming with belongings.

"I'm making coffee," she mumbles.

"Can I borrow the car?" I ask. I walk after her to the kitchen, already tying my shoes.

"We need to get those taillights fixed," she says. "You should ask Ben to. Are you going to see him?"

"What? Mom. Why would you ask me that?"

She looks down at the handwarmers I'm still holding onto tightly. She looks at my phone, my route to the law office already mapped out. It's been so long, I doubt I remember how to drive there.

"Why don't you just tell him you still love him? Please? Would you do that for me?"

"What? First of all, because I'm not a psycho. How desperate do you think I am?" I ask.

"I dare you," she chimes.

"And second," I continue, loudly, so she knows I'm ignoring her. "That's not what this is about." I shake the handwarmers at her. "And even if it was, Ben is a grown man, and I'm a grown woman, and we can do whatever the hell we want without our parents' opinions getting in the way, thank you."

"I agree," she says with a smile.

I scoff. "You always hated Ben. Why did you even invite him to your party in the first place?"

"I told you. I ran into him and you know how my old mouth blabs on and on sometimes, and next thing I know, he is invited. And I never hated Ben."

"Dad sure did."

"Dad didn't love that you were dating a Catholic. That's different than hating Ben."

I roll my eyes and she hands me the keys.

Ben was always the type of guy who said he went to school in Massachusetts, when he could have just as easily specified that it is Harvard University that he holds two degrees from. I was always the girl who wanted to please everyone, the girl who only knew how to feel fiercely. Now I am the woman who tries to care less, knowing we are all optimists when love is dangled within our reach.

After shipping myself away, I found that I needed a distraction in order to get over Ben. With so many people walking in and out of your life when your permanent residence is the sea, it wasn't difficult to find a fling. There was Sam, the Aussie I fell for during month three and remained pen pals with religiously for three weeks, and then just whenever it was convenient. Then there was Noah, a physicist from Detroit who loved art and tried to teach me about it. Kory, the slightly older man, Don, the slightly younger one. I played around with age gaps for a while. Maybe because I wanted so desperately to understand what being a grown-up meant.

I missed so many things. I missed hypothetical adult friends I never even had. I missed folding laundry with my mom; holding the freshly washed towels against my chest and welcoming their fleeting heat, the lavender scent my clean blouses used to carry. On the ship I always smelt of Clorox spray and sometimes alcohol, the kind for rubbing and the kind for drinking.

Sometimes I even convinced myself that I missed my fake husband—Keith. But I didn't miss him. I missed a world where he'd play Dad and I'd play Mom and we'd buy a casserole dish and both of our first cookbooks. We'd go to Home Depot on the weekends, shifting through paint sample cards until we found one that looked like us, and everything would be OK because it had to be. Most of all, we'd find you. And we'd bring you home.

But whenever I played this fantasy in my mind, it wasn't really Keith there with me. It was always Ben.

Chapter Twenty-One: Evie

What we have on our hands is a crown fire. The mountain people, like the Rileys, know it as the quickest of chaos. A natural disaster. It starts with one single flame and spreads in the hands of the wind, skimming the tops of trees at a rapid speed. This is how this particular flame multiplied into a wildfire. This is how a natural disaster began in Spring Mountains.

When lightning strikes, the earth can go ablaze. Or the ground, thirsty and in the midst of a drought, can seduce and encourage the sun and the heat.

Sometimes the earth mourns the dead things— the dead leaves, the dead twigs, the dead trees. Or perhaps the earth needs to shed itself of the dryness, like the peeling of damaged skin or the shedding of a snake's scales.

Whatever the reason, if there is one, the world can sometimes warm itself up enough to spontaneously combust and ignite.

We call it a natural disaster because we don't know what else to say, and we must say something. But to some degree nearly all wildfires are started wordlessly. By a human.

~

"Do you know my mother?" I ask into a peculiar hue of quietness. The evening news is going on mute from Mr. Riley's iPad, a color-coded map of the county with flame icons skipping across the screen. The evacuation border has been pushed another few miles, just east of the Riley home. Mitchell and I sit with this stranger on the floor and I can hear the crickets outside, same as I have most other nights from the few corners of the world I've witnessed.

"Can't say that I do," Mr. Riley replies. "What did you say her name was?"

It takes every ounce of courage I have to ask this man what I'm doing here in his house and I'm immediately flustered when I do. I am not sure if he knows that I attacked his son. Attacked poorly, sure, but still. I'm too ashamed to think about it.

I pull out the thinning newspaper clip and hand it to him.

"Joyce?" he starts. "Joyce, would you come out here, please?"

She does and Mr. Riley asks, "Have you seen this?" He hands her the piece of paper, discolored and curling at the ends.

"Oh, yes," she says. "I have the same one."

"You do?" Mr. Riley turns and looks at his wife. I realize he doesn't do that very often.

Mrs. Riley looks beautiful in a nontraditional sense; her hair is tussled slightly, and her clothes are simple but fresh, solid tones of violet and dark blue that make her eyes pop. Her thigh-length cardigan slumps down one of her sides, revealing a freckled, sturdy shoulder. Her large eyes flutter open and shut in full blinks.

"Who are you?" I finally ask. I can feel Mitchell leaning forward beside me.

"We're the Rileys," says Mrs. Riley.

"We knew each other," I say. "Right?"

"No, no. We have never met," says Mr. Riley.

The winds are howling now, violently so. The windows shake. Nobody pays any of it any attention.

"We were looking to adopt," Mrs. Riley continues as she pulls out the bracelet from her back pocket and shows me a charm in the shape of a teal ribbon. "I'm twenty-five years strong. After I got my ovaries removed."

I take back the newspaper clip.

"So this is?" Mrs. Riley mutters, pointing at the clipping, then at me. I hear all the unfinished versions of that same question. *You must be? Does this mean? How did you?*

Nobody says anything. The evening news is unmuted and the only other sound is that of Mrs. Riley's knee cracking as she eventually crouches down on the floor by her husband for a better view of the screen. I can almost hear the buzz of questions and answers coming together in Mitchell's head.

Mrs. Riley seems to be afraid to look at us, Mr. Riley is restless. He gets up to grab some of the paper cups stashed on top of the couch, which is currently impossible to actually sit on given the mountain of supplies resting in a heap on top of it. He politely offers us water; Mitchell and I are both polite enough to refuse.

Uncomfortable, I can't think of a way to get out. But honestly, I don't even want to get out. I want to belong here, next to a survivor mother and a middle-aged father that gets too riled up about the news channel buffering, in a house with matching furniture and color-schemed bedrooms.

I wonder if there are ways to mend myself to fit into this Riley mold. Surely, it is one that fits many locks. I even think of sending Mitchell back home. He will want to go soon, now that the Rileys have spoken. I want to be enveloped by all of them—the Rileys, Jessie and her father, Mitchell, even Hannah. I supposed even I, the introvert, get lonely sometimes.

~

I'm not able to see the flames outside the window until nighttime falls. Despite the frantic need to pile all the outdoor and flammable indoor furniture into the center of the house and away from the windows, the Rileys all sleep in their respective bedrooms, as per usual. The lower level of the home is now calm and still. What's left is the sounds of normalcy, despite the damage raging outside. The flames seem very far away so I wonder if it makes sense to be afraid.

When it comes to sleeping arrangements, it is clear that Mitchell and I are a burden. After some walking around in circles, Mr. Riley thinks to pull out two of the lawn chairs and lean the recliners down into flat beds. Mitchell's bare feet stick off the end and his head is hidden beneath the thin flannel blanket he is given. I pile up the rest of the blankets Mr. Riley found buried away in the coat closet and try to stay warm.

Despite all the preparations, I can't sleep. I sit up on my knees, sight pressed against the window, sure that I mustn't look away.

He never says it, but Mitchell thinks we've overstayed. I don't know what it is about this house, but it seems however I'm perceived here will reflect onto the rest of the world, and if I leave, I'm giving up.

I realize I haven't seen the upstairs yet. The place where the Rileys sleep, read news stories from their phones to each other right before bedtime, dress for job interviews or science project presentations at school. I have to get up there. I have to see if this place is for real. But my heart is pounding *no*s. *No, no, no, you shouldn't. It is not your staircase to climb.*

But it should have been.

Here I go. Here I come.

Slowly, I enter the perfect counterpart to the downstairs. Instead of a homey touch, everything is so elegant. The hardwood hallway floor is well polished, a half-circle of a side table grips the wall below a silver-lined oval mirror and holds a tall vase of sunflowers. Rows of oil-painted artwork of fruit and rolling hills hang from the walls. Each reddish-brown door is shut for the night. I'm afraid to touch anything.

When Matty coughs, I almost wet myself. *For fuck's sake*. He's slamming one of the perfect reddish-brown doors shut again behind him, walking around in a towel wrapped around his hip, texting, or something, on his phone. He surprises me when he leaves his bedroom door open. He mustn't have seen me.

And then, voices:

"I don't like strangers coming into our house like this, Joyce,"

"Would you try to keep your voice down? They'll hear us talking about them."

Freezing, blushing in a way as if they are looking straight at me and my reinvented childhood, there is nothing left to do but lean in and listen.

"What does she want? Money? A lawsuit?"

I imagine Mr. Riley pacing, running a hand through his thinning hair.

"A lawsuit? This isn't our fault, Ed."

"How could you invite them inside in the first place? Strangers in our home. They need to go. We don't owe them anything. Let them figure out how to get back to where they came from on their own."

"And by 'we' I suppose you mean me, right? I have to kick them out?"

Some more murmured back and forth. I'm not sure what to do. I look for some guidance. Matty. He is internalizing. Sitting in his corner, with his headphones resting on the outside of his ear, flinching once and then staring ahead in the way people do when they are avoiding something they've just seen from the corner of their eye.

Mrs. Riley sighs. "What else is new, Ed?" This time her voice is much quieter, but we can all still hear her.

Matty slips the right side of the headphone over his ear, but keeps the left half off. I mimic his noiseless movement and manage enough footsteps to exit this intimate family moment. I thank him in my head, and feel a twinge of guilt. Afterall, he is a Riley, too.

Mrs. Riley never does tell us we have to leave. In fact, she is more charming than ever.

~

Sometimes, people would come in to look at us. Couples, usually, smiling with only their lips and staying within the confinements of our living room doorframe made for these temporary doorframe-leaners. They'd stay there for thirty minutes or so. Some asked Hannah lots of questions: *how we were doing in school, what our favorite subjects were, our hobbies, how long have we been here, what kind of medical attention does that one need, are the two very close?* Some preferred to make up their minds without very many words. Hannah would put a pot on for three teas after forty or so minutes occasionally, though rarely. The visits were usually much shorter. A few months later we'd see a new couple leaning in just the same spot. The doorframe-leaners.

I did watch an adoption once. I can't place the name of the girl, but she lived with us for maybe three weeks and was older than the usual adoptee, a long-legged, dangly and freckled ten-year-old. They wanted a girl to keep their other little girl company, after their four-year-old died of leukemia.

"Oh, we tried having our own," the mother kept repeating to Hannah, nodding without stopping once. "Even with our Amanda, it took us nearly two years to get pregnant." She had a mousy quality to her, short and jittery, with a hair bob that might have been one-size too big for her heart-shaped face. They were a perfect couple to adopt.

Most Californians are qualified to adopt, on paper. But Hannah told us, more than once, how it was still so hard for the single parents. The non-U.S. citizens. The poor.

I only remember two or three singles coming through, usually swift, asking less questions. They'd look so intently at the wallpaper of each room while Hannah gave them a quick tour, you may have thought they were unsure of how they ended up here, in this foster home, looking for what?

Example: a middle-aged woman with a peculiar face came by several times. Mysterious, that's the word. Sporadic visits. She always wore her hair up in a bun. I never saw her in pants or skirts, dresses only.

As you'd expect, several visits to a foster home within a few weeks of each other usually leads to an adoption, or at least a home change. This one was never serious about any of us; she was just fascinated. Leaning against the doorframe with her arms crossed, hardly ever making an attempt to pretend that she was listening to a word Hannah was saying, or sometimes sitting on the edge of our living room couch with her hands folded neatly in her lap as to not disturb anything, studying us like pieces of abstract art in a museum.

I think she made Mitchell nervous and Hannah irritated. Hannah hated wasting already scarce time on window shoppers. I threw in a few eye rolls once I learned how to for their approvals. But this woman had this non-judgmental stare. I liked that.

When she stopped coming, I knew the three of us were wrong all along. She was smarter than the rest of them. Visiting foster homes as a fly on the wall, she wasn't blabbing about her own situation the way the others did, a defense, an explanation for being here at all. She simply watched us until she knew us. Until she picked someone, the right one, swept a foster child away and wiped that awful title gone with a new last name and a bedroom in a home with a mother, and a father, a pet dog, and a treehouse in the backyard.

Chapter Twenty-Two: Charlotte

Something unexpected happens when I walk into Wagner & Associates after all of this time. Overwhelming desire. There is nothing I want more than to sit down at a cubicle, bury myself in research, and show off my work at the end of the day.

I ask for Ben at the front desk. The office manager is someone new. He brings me to Ben's office and excuses himself quickly. Ben and I stand around his desk instead of in the nice lobby surrounded by flowers and office wall art, where I pictured this run-in to be.

"This is a lovely surprise," he says and crosses his arms over his chest. "What can I help you with?"

Before I get a chance to say a word, Ben's phone is ringing again.

"I swear, I'm never this popular," he says apologetically as he leaves me to check on his next surprise guest.

From the small crack between the blinds of Ben's office window, I can tell that she is pretty.

She has long black hair that swings lightly between her shoulders every time she tilts her head. She does that a lot when she speaks.

In an embarrassing sort of way, I'm grateful that she shows up when she does. What was my plan? To confess my love just because I found something that reminded me of him from so long ago? I pull the handwarmers out of my purse and stuff them into the front pockets of Ben's coat, resting over the back of his chair.

"I'm sorry, Charlotte," Ben starts. He's squinting back towards the lobby as he shuts the door behind him. "What was it that you wanted to talk to me about?"

"Oh, I, gosh." I search quickly for a new explanation. "This is awkward of me, I'm sorry. I was here to ask if you needed any help…around the office."

"Around the office?"

"Yeah, you know. Filing, research, all that stuff. I know it's been a while, but I'm sure I've still got it. And I'll need a job eventually." I clear my throat. "Thought I'd ask for old times' sake."

He doesn't smile at that last bit like I hoped he might. "Oh," he says instead. "Of course. Um." He looks around his desk. "Let me think about what we've got going on."

"Forget it. I shouldn't have asked."

"No, really, Char. I'll ask around."

~

"Do you think it was irresponsible of me to quit the cruise job?" I ask my mother one day. We're sitting by the fire. It's not cold out, but we figure we should use it one last time together. I'm holding an old copy of *Emma* in my lap. My mother is sitting on the floor with one of those adult coloring books. I look over at her twirling a light green coloring pencil between her fingers and smirk.

"Yes," she answers.

"*Mom.*"

"What? I'm being honest. It was irresponsible. You don't have to take everything so personally. You were smiling just two seconds ago when you asked. Should you really be asking me questions you don't want the answer to, then?"

"I was laughing at how ridiculous you look coloring. Am I supposed to take you seriously with that thing?"

"Yes. Yes, you are."

"You're the one who begged me to come out here," I mumble.

She sighs and puts the pencil down. "I'm not saying I don't think that it was the right thing to do. There's a difference. Doing the irresponsible thing isn't always a bad idea."

"That list has gotten to your head."

"Not at all. Everything had a purpose," she says proudly.

"Oh really? What was the purpose of cutting a goat's pubic hair?"

"Knitting taught us to give selflessly," she begins. "Karaoke taught us how to have fun in spite of ourselves. To not taking everything so seriously. Goats taught us how to step back from a situation where all we want to do is jump in and fix what we think is broken. Can't you tell now that not everything is so broken after all?" When I don't answer, she continues. "Don't you feel that now you know a little bit more about how life can be?"

"Mom." All I can manage for a few moments is to blink at her. "This is all such *Eat Pray Love*, feng shui bullshit."

"You feel like you've failed. At pretty much everything. That's why you're still thinking about a job that you hated. Is that right?"

"Well. It's not wrong. I am thirty-six years old and still—"

"You need to stop counting," my mother interrupts me. "Age doesn't change anything unless you let it. And you're not even old, so please." She points to a gray spot in her hair. "Stop crying about it."

"I know that, Mom. But just maybe. Maybe if I went to college. And got a different career. And got married. If only I didn't ruin…if everything got back on track." I sniffle, roll my eyes at myself, and wipe my nose with my sleeve. My sweater smells like the cinnamon latte I had this morning and the same lavender detergent my mother's been using since I was a kid.

"Then what? So what?" she asks.

"Well. I'd have enough money to have my own place like a God damn adult, for one. I'd be living a normal life. Finally. I wouldn't have to think about such stupid things like, if only—"

"If only you didn't get pregnant?"

My mouth drops a little bit. We never say the "P" word. It sits comfortably on her lips.

"You're so focused on what happened to you. What went wrong? Why you? What could you have done differently?"

I wait for an answer.

"It doesn't matter," she says and waves her arms at me like I'm about to miss something very important. "I'm sorry. It's the truth," she continues. "My point is, my dear, if you keep worrying about how you're a thirty-six-year-old screw up, don't be surprised when you end up an eighty-two-year-old screw up."

"So, stop thinking? That's your genius advice for me?"

"My genius advice is to stop thinking dumb. Think less if you'd like, sure, but think smart." She places a stack of very old college brochures in my hand.

~

I have never told anyone about this day. The luggage was all packed and waiting for departure by my parents' front door. A one-way ticket to Miami, where the first cruise ship set sail, was in my shirt pocket.

Since the moment I quit the paralegal job and accepted the cruise job in its place, I was on a one-track mindset. I knew a getaway had to happen. I couldn't explain why to anybody else. Wasn't everything okay again, finally? A world outside of this town wasn't something I knew well, and yet it was all I could see when I closed my eyes.

222

The day I left felt different. Less stable. I was sweating uncontrollably under my armpits, the back of my knees, my neck, in between my toes. My cheeks wouldn't stop burning. It felt as though I was constantly blushing, though I wasn't.

Three hours before my father planned to drive me to the airport, I swung my luggage on to its side on the living room carpet.

"What are you doing?" my mother asked from the doorway. She watched as I pulled the zipper open quickly and started lifting each layer of folded up clothing out one by one. "What are you looking for?" she asked again.

"I forgot something," I replied.

"What is it?" she asked. "What did you forget?"

"I'll know it when I still can't find it," I said. I couldn't let it go, that feeling that I was missing something terribly important.

She kneeled beside me and helped me shift through all of my neatly packed belongings.

By the time my dad walked in, I was throwing sweaters and stockings across the room, my mother running after each and refolding, begging me to let her make a trip to the corner store to get me whatever it is that I needed.

Dad was the one to zip up my bag, carry it back to its place by the door. He was never one for entertaining foolishness for the sake of my feelings, the way my mother would until the end of time.

"That's enough, Charlie," he said. "Enough acting like a child."

"Can I borrow the car?" I asked him hastily.

I didn't even know which adoption agency ended up taking you, after everything that happened. So I went to the closest one I could find. I sat in the chair by the side entrance where I was least likely to be noticed. I did nothing but stare at the loud ceiling fan for about an hour and a half.

There were no children while I was there. Hardly anyone at all, actually. A few stragglers that didn't seem to need much floated in and out.

Maybe they gave everyone away already. They must be good at their jobs. I made a promise to you, to anyone who'd listen, to be good at mine, too. That's all I had left to offer.

~

Something happened today. I wish I could tell you about it and that you would be proud; I signed up for the LSAT prep class. Perhaps, I hate to say it, this whole bucket list thing is not such a ridiculous idea after all.

Chapter Twenty-Three: Evie

Mitchell is beyond excited when I agree that we need to get going, fire or no fire. I hear him start the engine while I'm still at the front doorstep, adjusting and readjusting the different bag straps around my shoulders.

"Evie," Mrs. Riley says. "Could we chat?"

"Oh. Um." I look back at Mitchell in the car. He's too far away to hear us. "Sure? I guess so. What's up?"

"Did you want to come back in for this? Put those bags down?" she asks.

"I'm okay," I say and wait for her to look relieved. "What is it?"

"Your mother, well." Her voice goes quiet. She straightens up, rolls her shoulders back. Her chin is the last to make it up to me. "I know who she is. I saw her. Once."

"What do you mean?" Heat within me rises, and then dissipates. "Yes, I mean, of course. When you were thinking of adopting. You must have met."

"No, not just that—"

"Do you remember her name?" I ask.

Mrs. Riley shakes her head.

I shrug lightly and take a step back, towards the car.

"I mean more recently than that," says Mrs. Riley. "Afterwards. I saw her when we went to the adoption agency for Matty."

"Matty? What? Are you sure?"

She nods. "I am. Positive. I don't forget faces."

"Where is she? Where did you say you adopted him?"

"California. It was still back when we lived in California, in San Jose, just a few years after the first time we looked. She was just sitting there. But she didn't look…well."

"What do you mean?"

"Well. I sort of understand it," she says. "When you think you're going to have a baby, and then you don't. It's hard. It's still a loss."

Oh, your loss?

She doesn't know any better, I tell myself. I refrain from correcting her.

"I see," I say. "Thank you for telling me. And thank you for hosting us."

"I'm sorry—if I shouldn't have told you," she says. "I wasn't going to, I just—you deserve *something*."

I nod. What else is there to do? I nod, I get in the car with Mitchell, we drive home and listen to Blink 182 most of the way, and that's all there is of this.

~

"You're taking her word for it? Really?" Mitchell starts.

"Why not? She's the most normal. Out of all of them." Smiling to myself, I realize I feel bad speaking poorly of the Rileys. Any of them. As if they were my family for real.

"She gave you nothing. No name, no date. She said she sympathized with your biological mother's loss." Eye roll.

"She recognized her," I respond. "And she said it was when they were still living in San Jose. Where I was born. What are the chances?"

"Do you know how many people walk into adoption agencies every year in San Jose?" asks Mitchell. "That means virtually nothing."

It's late morning already and the highway is almost empty, just us and several trucks. Each one of them eventually disappears to a roadside rest area. The red and brown puffs of fog have either tumbled away or thinned out or drifted up. Ashes conceal the decaying land between the mountain peaks, the view a confusion of blurriness or just something that was once beautiful and has since been tampered with. Patchy. Unclear. It's not stuffy, but what's left of the smoke makes breathing feel bizarre—still manageable, but a very conscious process. The ground looks half-wild, half-groomed. Everything is bare and I look away.

"That woman she saw sitting there could have been anyone," Mitchell adds.

It's certainly a surprise. You at an adoption agency only a couple years after giving up a baby? It doesn't make any sense.

"Well," I start. "It does make some sense."

Mitchell snorts. "How?"

I don't answer. He tries again. "What do you mean by that?"

"Maybe she wanted a healthy baby," I say.

"Oh for fuck's sake," starts Mitchell. "You're healthy. You eat healthier than me, you're way smarter than me even if you don't think so, you could run circles around me if you wanted."

"What you and I say isn't the point. You know that," I say. "You have to admit it does make sense, doesn't it? If we're looking for a reason?"

Mitchell doesn't respond.

"Probably got herself a newborn," I say.

He starts fiddling with the radio.

We're going home. What you did years ago, after me, shouldn't matter. It won't help me find you. It won't change who I am.

You know it's so much more than all of this, though, right? It's you being there. "There" is so close to me, it turns out. An hour's drive away, all of this time.

It's a new life. Any life with you as a mother in it feels wrong.

~

"You still haven't spoken to Hannah since last time. When we were at the house, visiting. Have you?"

Mitchell is driving fast and quietly beside me. He will probably drive the entire way back, even as I keep offering to take over the wheel every hour or so.

"Nope," I answer. "Why? Did something happen?"

He doesn't answer.

"Any reason in particular I should have called her recently? Not her birthday, that's in June," I try. "We've been kind of busy."

"Stop being a smartass," Mitchell says. "Just call her."

~

I'm lucky to have a friend like Mitchell. I know this is true. Sometimes I wonder if I'm missing something by not forcing myself to experience the company of female friends. Like normal people. Strangers think we're a couple sometimes, not siblings. It's true that we look nothing alike, of course.

He must think that I've already fallen fast asleep. Everything is quiet and my eyes have been shut for a while now. My face is hidden beneath the sweatshirt I've been using as a blanket.

I had a funny habit when I was younger of placing my fully outstretched palm perfectly over my entire face, opening and closing my eyes. I enjoyed realizing the loudest thing in the world in that moment was my own breath. Lashes bending and brushing against my hand. I'd think of how the whole world was my eyes. Were the parts of the universe that were no longer visible to me when my hands covered my face still there, existing, behind my flesh?

I don't think I've changed much. I still obsess and think too much about the littlest things that don't seem to matter to other people. I wish I were still small. I'd hold my little hands over my face and scream, and see how many people on the other side could still hear me.

~

"Who do you keep texting?" I ask moments after we unlock our apartment door. It's cold in here, like we haven't been home for months.

"Huh?" Mitchell continues to stare down at his phone and heads for his bedroom.

"If that's Hannah, Mitch, I swear to God."

"Calm down. Not everything is about you."

~

I can't leave things at the door the way Mitchell does. I don't follow an out-of-sight-out-of-mind lifestyle. I watch as Mitchell exits our failed mission to get answers with a lightness I can never understand. I cradle my head in my hands and know there is no point in trying to fall asleep tonight.

Chapter Twenty-Four: Charlotte

The LSAT preparatory class meets three times a week at the local community college. The faculty and the other students describe the course as jam-packed. Short but intense, stressful, probably rewarding. For me, it's a breath of fresh air. A challenge. I consume myself with it.

I even make some friends. Most of the other students are just out of college. Your age. A small group of us starts meeting after class at a nearby coffee shop. There, we pass the prep book around and take turns testing each other, question after question after question.

"I swear, they come up with these tests to knock the sense out of us," mutters Max into his large cup of black coffee. He has thick glasses that are too big for his head and make his pupils look ginormous. "It's mind games. Why don't they just give us a series of riddles and call it a day? Mad libs? Maybe my two-year-old nephew should come up with some questions?"

"What's colorful, can't move but can look at you, and never gets old?" Deborah pipes up.

"I wasn't actually interested in hearing a riddle," mumbles Max.

"A mirror?" guesses Preetika.

"Not colorful," says Deborah.

"It could be," challenges Preetika.

"When I first met you, you could barely stomach hot chocolate without whipped cream," I say to Max with a smug smile as he chugs the rest of his coffee. "Amazing what a few weeks of hard work can do to us."

We each rededicate ourselves to our books.

"What's this?" Preetika pokes at the slim booklet in my hands. The study group has been paying extra attention to me ever since I mentioned in passing that I was thinking of picking up a part-time job of some sort once my mother leaves town. They were unamused. *Studying is a full-time job*, they keep telling me.

I flip the booklet up so that they can see the cover. "I'm actually studying for another test, too," I say.

"CLEP? What's that?"

"College-Level Examination Program," I pause. "Because. I never finished college. So, I need to pass it before applying to law schools," I finish.

"What do you mean? Like you never got your bachelor's degree?" asks Deborah.

"You didn't graduate?" Preetika asks at the same time.

"That's right," I say.

Blank stares.

"My mom got her MBA while I was working on undergrad at Berkeley," Max says eventually.

When I was growing up, I was always taught that there is one single path for each of us that we are destined to take. Now people like to tell me that there is no such thing as age-defining aspirations. No "timeline" for things. I wonder which is the truth.

Don't get me wrong, I understand the world my classmates are living in. I know the place well, though I am only a visitor there now.

They live like this test defines their lives because, well. Right now it does for them. It's their truth. The path we were destined for. That's how I grew up understanding the world, too. Follow the rules—all of them—and the universe will be on your side.

I have to smile when Max dramatically throws a fistful of pencils up in the air when he answers the last five questions in a row incorrectly and says that this is it, he is quitting.

"It's too late to change your mind, Max," says Deborah solemnly. "You picked law. What else are you going to do with political science?"

"You could just be a paralegal," says Preetika. It's a joke but no one laughs. They get quiet and decide it's time to call it a day.

As we walk out together, I look over at Deborah. "What's the answer?" I ask her. "To that riddle."

"A portrait of a person," she says. We're alone now, so she looks at me and says, "I know this is random. But for what it's worth, I think it's great that you're going back to school. Following your dreams and stuff. I wish more people would. How's that for changing the world?"

~

On Saturday morning, I help my mother pack the few clothes she'll be taking with her to Europe. That is, we contemplate how much summer and how much winter clothing she will need, give up and throw a few pairs of shoes and toiletry into an open suitcase on the floor. We make plans to drop off the rest of her boxed-up belongings for storage.

I try to at least fold things up neatly to make the most of the little space she'll have to hold all of her things. Meanwhile, my mother sits cross-legged with her laptop on her armchair where she usually reads before bed, and believe it or not, she does something that surprises me yet again. She asks me if I'd consider creating an online dating profile for myself. Maybe the both of us will do it. Just for fun. Because why not?

"Absolutely not," I answer.

"Why not? Everyone uses these things these days," she says.

"It's not the online part, it's the dating part," I say. "And if I ever were to create one. Don't you think it's a little pathetic to have my mom set one up for me?"

She tries talking about time. Falling in love, starting a family, starting a new career—it's all still in the cards for me, if I want it. Nodding at me nonstop. Is she trying to console me?

"You'll find someone," she likes to say to me. This time her voice is crystal-clear about its intent to console me.

Trying not to laugh out loud, I volunteer to drop off the scarves we've made for donation. Each scarf is already rolled up into a swelling spiral of fluff, different shades of greens, dark pinks, and blues peeking out from three large garbage bags. It is a windy day and I am trying to get the overstuffed bags to fit into the trunk of my mother's car.

"Need help?" His voice gets to me before I see him standing at the end of the driveway.

"Are you sure?" I reply in between breaths and full body shoving of the thin material still bulging out of the trunk. "This could be a fulltime job."

He shrugs and says, "I'm great with jigsaws."

Ben starts to twist and turn the bags with delicate and gentle hands. He smells like faint cologne and coffee. Yes, I do halt all my huffing and puffing long enough notice.

"Looks like you've found a way to stay busy," he starts.

"Were you headed somewhere?" I interrupt.

"Just taking a long lunch." He's not in his lawyer-man suit and tie today. He's dressed for a grocery run or somewhere along those lines. My cardigan swings unnaturally around my thighs with the unwelcome wind.

"I'm not hitting on you," he adds, putting his hands up innocently. I must be mean mugging him. "I'm here on business."

"*Business*, huh?"

"My ex-wife's brother runs a travel agency. Sales, customer service, marketing, all that stuff. I told him about you—"

"You did?"

"Well. Yes," Ben stutters, continues. "Actually, she came to visit me the same time you did. Ian left his soccer cleats at the office while visiting, so she had to pick them up before practice. So, it was top of mind for me. Must have been fate. Anyways."

Ah. The woman with the beautiful black hair. Good taste, Ben.

"What about filling a position as a desk rep?" he asks. "Lots of admin work and reorganization. The whole system needs a facelift. Will make you want to rip your eyes out, not for the faint of heart. But they pay well, I hear, and hours are flexible. They're pretty excited about your hospitality experience, obviously. That is, if you're here to stay."

I'm touched. Honestly, I forgot he even offered to ask around. I invite him inside for a quick cup of coffee. I tell him about law school. Well, law school one day. He congratulates me.

A few minutes later, Ben's iPhone buzzes twice—a reminder of another appointment in thirty minutes.

"It's the weekend," I remind him. "Do you always have that thing on?"

"Better get going," he says in between loud gulps, finishing up the last few drops of his coffee and leaving the mug beside the sink.

I follow him to the doorway where he wiggles into his loafers and zips his jacket up halfway. We face each other. For a moment, I'm terrified that he will try to kiss me. My heart drops when he doesn't.

He clears his throat and says something polite. We chat for a little while longer.

"What happened to us, Ben?" I ask as a laugh between the two of us fizzles down, a memory—something about an early morning when we got caught by security kissing in the company parking lot so long ago seems hilarious again. He looks surprised, confused by the question.

I smile and shake my head. This tragedy is mine, and mine alone.

"Oh, before I forget." He reaches for something in his coat pocket. I grin, remembering the handwarmers.

He pulls out a small bulb instead. "I'll fix your taillight later."

"What?" He must have noticed the handwarmers by now. Did he even remember that he gave them to me once? "You don't have to do that," I snap. Roll my eyes. Stare at him. "You don't have to keep doing this. I don't need you to save me. Or pity, or whatever this is. You know that, right?"

"Charlotte," he starts with a frown. "Why are you getting upset? I'm just trying to help."

"I don't need your help. I didn't ask for it."

"You did. You asked for my help getting a job. Your mother mentioned the taillights again—"

I shake my head. "Have you been this way with my mother the entire time that I was away? At her beck and call?"

"Jesus, Charlie. I did this for you. Just forget it."

"It's not my fault that I left." I put my hand on the doorknob to stop him from walking out. "That's what people do when they grow up, they leave."

He laughs at this. "Is that what growing up is?"

I burn as he shakes his head slightly. He's right. What do I know?

"I wasn't trying to kiss you earlier," he says as he takes a step closer to me. "I know you thought that's what I was doing, I could tell. This isn't what I came here for." He slips his hand on the small of my back, pulls me closer to him. "I want you to know that."

I can feel his body heat hovering over me now. Still feels like Ben. He slips his fingers under my chin, tilts my head up, leans in. His kisses still taste the same, his lips are salty. His breath gives me shivers. Yeah, same old Ben.

I don't want this to end. But my feet are jittering, aching to run. It's a feeling I know well.

I knew I wasn't loving correctly at nineteen when every time I tried to say, "I love you," something knocked the voice out of me, a block of muteness in my way. The block was so heavy, I could almost see it. Every time I got to thinking that maybe I wasn't a complete coward, it'd roll its ugly four corners back in and keep my mouth shut.

Ben looks at me expectedly, now, but I just push his arm away from where he's still holding me around my waist.

Now, more than anything in the world, I want to throw that foolish block of muteness away. I want to tell Ben everything, everything there is to know about you, and me, and you and me together, and him and me together.

Sometimes we want to improve. And we put all of ourselves into this self-improvement project—we read the literature, we step out of our comfort zone, we sign up for LSAT classes, or the online dating profiles. I believe that when we look back at it all, the change is there. A steppingstone. It is all worth it. Change happens all of the time, even for the frightened, defeated hearts.

But today? Today I failed. I threw Ben's protective arm away from me and I ran like hell, opening the door for him wordlessly and slipping the bulb back into his palm.

Chapter Twenty-Five: Evie

They say rock bottom brings a sense of clarity. It makes you wonder if positivity was always just a bogus act. As I sit in Alice's office with a pack of ice held over my right eye, I wonder if I have indeed hit rock bottom.

As promised, I am prepared to drive Jessie to her ballet class after swim lessons. But they never show up. They will never show up again, it turns out. They are moving away—she, her brothers, her dad, and her mom. Jessie's mom filed for divorce, then agreed to try marriage counseling and a new home instead, in Portland. My day is now free and Alice places me on arts and crafts duty.

Have you heard of the spitball challenge? Essentially, kids make their usual spitballs—roll a piece of paper into a ball, chew on it for a while to get it sticky, all of that. They shoot it off a straw to give it more distance. Distance is the challenge. Lately, the older kids have taken to making a dartboard out of the construction paper we use for crafts sometimes and shooting spitballs at it. The closer to the center of the poorly drawn circle in the middle, the more points you get. It's usually a nuisance, running after them to stop it, cleaning up. But today is different. Today I find the whole shenanigan hilarious.

We sit cross-legged on the cold floor, myself and a few of the kids, shooting spitballs off the balcony overlooking the parking lot.

When I step on the skateboard so conveniently hidden behind me and hit my head on the door, I laugh. It is funny. That's how I end up here. Now I want to melt behind this icepack and disappear. The old, lumpy throw pillows on the loveseat in Alice's office poke at my back and prevent me from dosing off.

"Did something happen?" Alice asks. "While you were away?"

The answer is no. Nothing at all.

I thought I was doing better. You thought so, too, right? I am not equipped for getting over things, it turns out. There is so much more up and down to it than anyone ever prepares you for, in this 'getting over' business.

"Am I in trouble?" I ask.

"Are you five years old?" Alice responds.

I laugh. "That's something I would say."

~

Mitchell's interest in my past continues to fade. We haven't talked anymore about the Rileys, or about all that wasted time we spent waiting for the practitioner, or how lucky we were that the woman at the adoption agency made a mistake, or anyone or anything. I am relieved for this. I really am. The things about each other we can count on never changing.

That is, of course, until I understand the real reason for Mitchell's strange behavior lately. The secret texts and a little too much enthusiasm about getting back home. Mitchell tells me about the new girlfriend he has been keeping a secret for the past few weeks. The news he figured he should wait to tell me until I sorted through all of my crap.

Though I'd hardly describe my crap as now sorted, Mitchell must get impatient. He tells me he'd like me to finally meet her.

At the local Italian restaurant we usually get takeout from, we sit outside because New Girlfriend doesn't like how close together the tables are inside. Her voice is shrill, and she hardly lets Mitchell or me get a word in. Mitchell doesn't seem to mind.

Talkers. I focus on breadsticks instead. What else is there to do? *For the love, where is my lasagna?*

She is talking about her new project, starting a catering service with her father. Then, about her trip to Vietnam with her two sisters. Then, about volunteering with her special ed class back when she was in high school; she planned group trips for them. Field trips. Overnights. She's good at planning trips.

"And that's when I told him, 'No way. If the handicapped kids aren't going to get to ride the steamboat back to the village, then neither will I.' It just isn't fair that the normal kids get to do whatever they want."

She nods, wordlessly deciding that this is the topic. This is what we're going to bond over. I cock my head at her. Is she the normal one?

She asks me what I do for work.

"How are those swim lessons going?" Mitchell asks after I answer.

New Girlfriend looks surprised when Mitchell tells her I've been swimming every day for years.

"Wow! You're such a badass," she says with a smile. "Such an inspiration."

They go on to tell me about what they've been up to. A beach day. Picnics every Thursday. Documentaries. Learning how to skateboard. Building homes overseas, or at least they'd like to.

"Are you for real?" I finally ask when she leaves us for the ladies' room to freshen up.

"What, volunteering in Mexico? I know. It was a crazy, last minute idea. Hers, actually. That's one of my favorite things about her. She's so spontaneous."

"Can you hear yourself right now? You sound pathetic. You're goo-goo ga-ga. This isn't you."

"This is what people do. It's called being normal, Evie." He scratches his head.

Silently, I pick at the lasagna noodles on my plate.

I know what you think. I decided not to give this girl a fair chance before I even met her. I'm hating her for nothing else but inconvenient timing. Or a slip of a tongue. A poor choice of words. My own over-the-top sensitivity to a word that describes me well. I know, I know. I don't have to confess to anyone that I need Mitchell to be here, present, focused, with me, until I feel better. Like he used to. And she has gotten in the way. But, come on. Look at her. Listen to her. She's not making it easy for me to be fair.

"It's being normal, and not feeling sorry for yourself all the damn time," Mitchell says. He has been thinking about this for a long time. Half of my lasagna is gone by now. "It's moving on from the crummy stuff. You should try it."

She is back at our table and hesitates before sitting down. Impressive. She does not strike me as someone who knows how to hesitate at all.

"Is everything OK?" she asks.

Mitchell mumbles one more "grow up," at me under his breath, but seems to cool down once New Girlfriend distracts him with conversation and the two ignore me for the rest of the meal.

Managing to muster some self-control and say thank you when Mitchell picks up the check, I wonder how rude it'd be to just slink off without another word or if that's what is expected of me.

~

End of the workday. Icepack still in hand, I walk home. *No more*, I promise myself. No more waiting, or searching, or whatever the hell I convinced myself I was doing up there, in between the smog and flames of the mountain village we would have never known existed if we hadn't gone looking for it, Mitchell and I.

Look for something new.

Faded sidewalk trees engulf me, my thoughts, my rain boots even though it's dry out and has been all week. A feeble breeze tries to push me along as I stand at the crosswalk and wait, watch the stream of cars rush by.

A new hobby. Doesn't matter what. That's what I'll do.

~

When you're born with something like cerebral palsy, the support groups are endless. They haven't always been. They are important. Of course they are. But there's something that happens when you start to make up groups like that. Socially. People naturally clique up. You have to decide. Are you part of the group, or not? You can't be in both worlds.

I didn't want to decide. Why should I have to? It seemed strange, to categorize ourselves as different all of the time, on purpose. To tout it. So I continued to go. And I continued to resist. And, as it turns out, when you try to be in two worlds at once you end up not really belonging in either one.

Our social worker thought transferring me into the special ed class at school might be a good alternative to the support groups I was having trouble connecting with. Where life is supposed to be made a little bit more accessible to us.

Four weeks in and I was already getting bored of the new class. I was getting restless. But then things changed. I made a friend. His name was Peter and he was one of those people bursting with positivity. Humbly bursting, not the annoying kind.

"I hate being in special ed," I confessed to him one day. We were sitting on the same side of a lunch table outside, just the two of us, watching a bunch of kids on the playground.

"You're lucky you have the choice," said Peter.

I shrugged. "I don't really."

"Sure you do," responded Peter. "You can walk, jump, play…"

We both flinched as a rubber kickball soared in our direction. Then we remembered what we were talking about. We both looked away.

A small part of me really wanted to grab him by the shoulders and shake him. *Look around, you goofy kid*, I wanted to say, *you're just as free as I am if you let yourself see it*.

About ten minutes later, a bully managed to make it to the special ed wing. He thought it'd be funny to steal Peter's wheelchair and go running with it. With Peter still inside of it, obviously. I was still sitting right next to him and didn't know what to do. I ran, but I wasn't as fast as that kid.

What's the point of being able to run if I can't keep up? I wanted to ask Peter. But he was too far away, and by the time I caught up with him, a teacher had already intervened.

The teacher led an unharmed and still-good-spirited Peter back to the classroom. I was too ashamed to even sit next to him for the rest of the day.

I told Hannah that I didn't want to be in the special ed class anymore, and she called the district just like I asked her to. I was high functioning enough that no one gave it too much thought. There was a waitlist to consider, after all.

I said being there felt like more of a distraction from my studies than anything else. Too much going on. But you know the truth. Feeling disabled—it's not something I feel very often. Not anymore. It's something I strive not to feel every day.

Chapter Twenty-Six: Charlotte

My mother and I toss the last of the old kitchen dishes into my own move out pile, a cardboard box my mom labels as "For Donation" with a smirk. We check the expiration date on her passport one more time and laugh about how we both misread it as two years ago instead of three years from now and panic at the same time.

We officially hand over the key to the new family moving in tomorrow. It is no longer our home to live in.

I've decided to stay in town. I have my test to think about. My future life. Mom offers to call off the deal and let me stay at the house, but I decline. "I don't need so much space," I tell her. "And I should find something new for me."

We drive to the airport together with soft rock on the radio and not a lot of cars on the highway. It isn't rush hour yet.

Mother sits next to me and we give each other a tearful sort of goodbye smile when I pull up by her gate. We look around the familiar airport and can't believe we just drove away from the building we both called home for so long.

"I'll call you when I land. I'll call you every Sunday. Call me if you need anything," she says.

"I'll be fine. You'll be fine. We'll all be just fine," I respond.

"That's my girl," says Mom.

Here, outside the airport, there is a man. Because, of course, there is always a man. He catches my eye as he climbs into a cab with his collar half popped up the way it must always be after a long day of work, and I could swear this man is Ben.

I know, of course, that it isn't.

Regardless, my heart is pounding. This look-a-like must have just landed, a quick daytrip for work perhaps. In my head, this version of Ben walks right up to me, asks if we can talk and it makes me sad because I want so desperately for this to be real. It is too late now.

I help my mother unload her carry-on from the trunk when I notice her left eyebrow is by her hairline at this point. "Did you hear what I said?" she asks after waving her passport in front of my face.

"Sorry," I say. "Yes, I'll send you a photo of the new apartment as soon as I set it up."

"Thank you," she answers. "But that's what I asked you ten minutes ago. The last time you weren't paying attention." A smirk dances on her lips. "Why don't we assign each other one more bucket list item as a parting gift, just for old time's sake?"

"Sounds more like a dare. Not an extension to the bucket list," I say. I check the time. I'm supposed to meet Deborah at noon for the key to our new place. My new apartment. Deborah's roommate, luckily, moved out right around the time Mom got the offer on the house.

"Don't correct your mother," she says. She hands me a neatly folded up piece of binder paper, pulls me in for a tight squeeze, and kisses my cheek. "We'll talk soon," she says. "Think of what you want to add to my bucket list by then and I'll add it to my itinerary."

I stay to watch her through security for no reason at all besides that I don't have much else I care to do today. The realization of how much I'll miss her weighs me down and meeting Deborah is no longer enough motivation to get going.

Until I see what is on the inside fold of this piece of paper, scribbled out in neat, curvy letters and numbers. My final bucket list item.

~

It takes her about two and a half days to realize that I'm following her. Maybe the yellowed headlights I declined to get cleaned at the carwash last week for an extra eleven dollars gave me away.

She's captivating in an average way. Medium height and extraordinary posture that makes the way she walks stand out in a crowd, eyelashes that must be long because they are noticeable if she blinks a bunch while standing in profile.

In retrospect, I must have known that she wasn't really you. Maybe that's why I kept following her, that midafternoon after waiting behind the steering wheel in the parking lot of my old community college campus. My heart sped up because she was carrying one of those small birthday balloons on a stick that you can buy at the supermarket and I decided this had to be you. It just had to be. Look at her.

She ended up giving the balloon to someone else, but I ignored it.

I wasn't planning on speaking to her. But then I saw her weeping, behind a small window of a house near campus after class when she thought no one was watching and I got so worried. It comes so fast, the worry.

I devised a speech in my head. I even wrote some parts down on paper so I wouldn't forget it. A bright orange notepad I found in the glove compartment curled around the wheel so I can write against some surface. I must have sat there jotting for hours.

The words were useless. I never did say anything to her. The policewoman with the tight smile tapped at my window much before I figured out a way to embarrass myself. My plan to throw some advice at this young woman without telling her who the hell I even was. She was so close to me. You were. Who knew.

Chapter Twenty-Seven: Evie

My newest obsession is energy. Energy drinks, caffeinated mints, exercise. I splurge and buy one of those cheaper stationary bikes—which I love. After tearing open the box it came in and setting it up by the living room window, it becomes clear that this is going to be my new favorite toy. Minutes turn to hours once I'm on those pedals.

"Sleep is for quitters," I say to Mitchell when he asks me if I'm going to bed soon. My energy is keeping him awake. I'm fast enough that it feels like I'm running. Running suspended in the air.

He rolls his eyes and goes back to his room. That's how we communicate, now. Just the minimum amount.

~

Alice recently bumped up my hours. The job is now my life. When I'm not working, I'm working out.

It feels as though I'm pedaling through the workday. I barely hear when Jessie says goodbye for the last time and Alice tries to have a real conversation.

"If something happened and you want to talk," Alice keeps saying.

I wonder how much she knows.

Jessie again, telling me thanks. Thanks for everything. The back of her father's head when I turn to say goodbye.

"What is it now, Alice?" I ask. She's hovering by me, following me all over the daycare center, like she has a secret she can't bear to keep.

"How long are you planning on working here?" she asks. When I give her a weird look, she explains, "Weren't you planning on going back to school? I thought you said that when you started."

"I can never understand you," I respond. "Didn't you just promote me?"

"It's just a question." She shrugs. "Don't get too comfortable. That's all."

Jessie leaves, and so do all the others. My day is done. A family that was never mine slips away and I see you. The version of you I've built up and perfected for so long. You're a hollow ragdoll. I get it.

~

On the stationary bike, I still don't know what Alice meant by that. Comfortable. When have I ever felt comfortable?

I watch as Mitchell pulls shirts and sweaters from his laundry basket, stuffs them into his backpack. He is spending the next week or so at Hannah's home, helping her get accustomed to life after her knee surgery. New Girlfriend will be joining, of course.

Hannah sent us a text the other day letting us know her surgery is scheduled for today. Mitchell volunteered to be the one to help her while she recovers. I did too, but it sounds like I am not needed.

"I got it," is all Mitchell says about it.

"I'm happy to help her out," I say. "You always do it. And I get how it is."

"I get it, too," Mitchell grumbles at me. Is he jealous that I understand what post-surgery feels like? Really?

I sigh. My calves are beginning to hurt. Pedaling faster makes it easier to ignore the pain. Push right past it. Works every time.

~

A memory. I'm ten years old and looking for something. Fruit snacks. The thinning grocery bag I used as a lunchbox was where I always kept it, in a crack between the bookshelf and the leg of the classroom coatrack. It wasn't pretty. Not the pinks and pale green polyester of the other girls' lunch bags. Not the animal print or the floral. But it worked. I quickly dug up my snack and stuffed the bag back into its hiding spot.

I never ate the fruit snacks. We'd get them every day for lunch and I'd always give them away. Not because I didn't like them. Because everybody else did.

When I was in special ed, I'd give it to Peter almost every time. Slip it into the pocket of his jacket. We never talked about it. But he knew it was from me.

I never said anything about it to anyone. I found a new person to grace with fruit snacks every day. The day Maya fell off the playground and cried, I gave it to her. The day Joey lost his tooth after getting hit in the face with a volleyball. There was always something, someone.

I think of this as I stare at the kids at my daycare job pull out their individual lunches. Will this be the rest of my life? It's not so bad. Not bad at all. I thought it would be different. Is your life as you planned it to be? Was it all worth it?

When I figured out who that kid was who ran off with Peter and his wheelchair, I gave him the fruit snacks every day of the week. His name was Toby. I gave it to him because I knew. I heard what happened when I was in the school office some other day, picking up a misplaced jacket from the lost and found. His mother who was sick in the hospital. And I felt bad for him.

I try to remember what it felt like to be so willingly forgiving.

~

And another. I'm eighteen. I have just had sex for the first time. It was okay. It did hurt, but not in the way I thought it would. He was a guy from my freshman orientation group. He held me up and tried to pull my legs into all kinds of positions that didn't feel right. Flexibility isn't really my thing. I got tired of telling him.

A few weeks later, I got a positive pregnancy test. Don't worry, it was false. Did you know aspirin can cause false positives sometimes?

255

I didn't freak out about that one over-the-counter test. I'm not new to inconsistencies. I'm not new to waiting for lab results. I know stuff happens. I went into the doctor's office and got tested. I wasn't pregnant.

One thing I was sure of right away, after seeing that plus sign on the stick, was that I'd get an abortion. If needed. I didn't have the money, but I'd figure it out.

I didn't know then about you, about us, remember?

So do you still believe that I don't get it? The worst part is that I do. I get it so well that it overwhelms me. It's tipped me over and I haven't been able to get back up ever since.

Lots of the things you saw, I probably saw them too. Protestors waiting on the streets. Signs about what the baby can do and hear at week six. You see your doctor sneak out the back door with her head down, running to her car. I do get it. Trust me. I'm a woman, too.

You're a hollow ragdoll, dangling, pushed and pulled, watching yourself act in a way that's not like you. Something that is not you at all. That's all I've been doing lately. I thought I was a survivor.

Chapter Twenty-Eight: Charlotte

I always thought that people just shed their own cluelessness one day. A pool of knowledge and wisdom just pours into us overnight, and that's when we outgrow our parents. For the first time, we'd have all the answers ourselves.

Here's a shocker: that never really happens.

When asked if I accept the international charges, I press "1" before the recording finishes. The note she slipped into my palm before she set foot on that airplane still irks me. We always took the easy way out, our family.

"Mom," I burst when I hear her voice, muffled and happily distant, like I woke her up from a good dream. "You knew where she was this whole time—both you and Dad—didn't you?"

She doesn't ask me who I am talking about. "Well, yes, Charlotte, of course I did."

"Why were you looking for her?" I ask, trying to keep my fume from fizzling out in comparison to her calm and steady voice. "How could you do that and not tell me, all of these years?"

"I had to make sure she was alright," Mom answers.

"I thought you knew nothing," I respond.

"Is that true?" she says back.

I don't want this two-minute outburst to be the end. And yet I can't think of another word to say. How hadn't I seen this all along?

"Charlotte," Mom starts again after a long silence. "I knew they wouldn't want her anymore. We all did. Waiting for her to die, like all the doctors were. It's something else."

Have you ever been surprised to hear your own voice? That's how I feel, at this moment, when I ask her what you are like. "Tell me everything you know."

"A real miracle," Mother says. "She truly is."

~

3:30 a.m.

I wake up thinking you've been ripped away from me again. It's been a while since I've dreamt of you, little one. In my dreams, we are the best of friends. A mother and daughter close in age, brushing each other's hair, laughing, watching romantic comedies together, talking about boys.

Maybe I'd keep all the sad stories to myself if I had raised you. I wouldn't want you to know heartbreak. I wouldn't want you to know what it means to despair. Maybe I'd want you to believe in everything with an open heart and earnestness, always, for as long as you can believe. Still making up your own happy endings. I wouldn't want to harm your perfection, the way adults do sometimes with the perfectly youthful.

4:30 a.m.

I am sweating through the sheets again. I hate that I still think I'm in that old house. I hate that ship. I hate every place I've ever had to sleep in. Sleep feels like hospital beds.

5:50 a.m.

I'm done closing my eyes against aimless body aches, it is already so hot in here. I open the window and for a second my heart lifts. It's quiet and still out there.

6:45 a.m.

Sometimes I feel like these thoughts are love letters to my memories. *Be safe*, I want to say, *safe far, far away from me*. Too far for you to hear me, how much distance do we need to stop the damage?

7:15 a.m.

I'm up. In my new home, the one I share with Deborah.

I watch as the yolk leaks through a little tear in the bread crust of my eggs in a nest breakfast. I've put on a dress and done my hair, now sitting on the uncomfortably tall stool by the kitchen counter. There's nothing more I want to do this morning than to run outside into an open world and yell as loudly as I can.

8:00 a.m.

Deborah comes into the living room, crying.

"You're awake," I say. "Oh, gosh. What's wrong?"

She hurries past me, throws herself onto the couch and clutches a throw pillow tightly to her chest. She shudders, then she roars. Agony is everywhere.

"Deb, what happened?"

She scoots over to let me sit beside her on the sofa, a big and cushiony couch we sink into slowly while we sit in silence. I let her cry, not asking her anything else.

"I don't want to be pregnant," she finally whispers. "I don't. I don't want it. I don't want to be pregnant."

She goes on to tell me about the missed period, about telling her boyfriend before she took the test, about how he disappeared, just like that, after dating for all of these years. Their fifth anniversary would be next month.

"He won't even answer my calls," she says. "I know he's reading my texts. He's a good texter."

"Oh, Deb," is all I say.

She tells me she's ashamed of all the years. All the years she wasted on him. "I let people think I'm so smart. But I'm no better than all of the other girls, doing stupid, mindless things. And for what? For a guy." Her shoulders slump.

"Don't do that," I say. "Didn't you like who you were when you were with him?"

She nods.

"You're still the same person you were when you were with him, all of that time. You still get to be that girl. That's the most important thing for you to remember now. You're still her when you're hurt and when you struggle and you'll get past this. It's what you do."

"He's probably afraid," she says. "He's probably upset that this happened."

"Forget about him for a second," I say. "He's removed himself. It sucks, but that's what today looks like. Tomorrow may look different. We don't know. Today, right now, with what you know and what you have, what's right for you? What's best?"

I'm surprised and silenced by a hug. She doesn't strike me as a hugger. Her arms fold lightly around my shoulders. I hold her and rub her back until she quiets down.

When I drive her to Planned Parenthood, I assume I will be staying in the car. But she looks at me expectantly and waits until I get out, walk her into the clinic, sit beside her in the waiting room. It's unexpectantly pleasant in here. Vases of pale peonies are all around, in between seats and on different corners of the long front desk. The people are nice and patient as we figure out the paperwork. Everything looks and smells so clean. I'd still rather be in the car.

"It'll get better sooner than you think," I say to Deb after her name is called and she looks at me with nervous, hopeful eyes.

I want to give her advice the way that mothers do. The way my mother does, whether I ask for it or not. Deborah is so young. You are even younger.

There is so much I want to say to you.

~

You.

I wish you understood how ripe your life is.

If only you understood. You'd treat each boring just-another-day as your very own amazing adventure bursting at the seams with possibilities. You'd dress up in your favorite clothes every day and stop curling your hair and throw away that cheap concealer you get that smells like paint because you're beautiful already and you'd know that. You wouldn't forget it. You'd trade in every moment you spend worrying about making the right move for moments that lead to even more moments, memories with the most important people in your life. You'd trade out words like fault for forgiveness. You'd be kinder to others, to yourself.

Sometimes I look back at my younger self and I am shocked at all one girl can lug around. You must be even stronger than me, with an even larger load on your back, as generation exchanges go sometimes. Day in and day out, from time spent running through the motions to lying in bed at night fluttering in and out of consciousness when you're so close to sleep—what are you worried about?

I know. You don't have to fear anything from the past. All that is over and done with.

Don't force positivity. It will come. Have hope for the future when it comes to the irreplaceable things. Don't fight yourself. Your life is right now. Every day, every minute. Don't ever forget it: don't fight yourself. I do this all of the time. Do not hate me, unless it serves you somehow.

I get jealous thinking of all the experiences you have before you, all of the amazing, delicious, bubbling life before you. The best kind of jealous, of course, the happy, nostalgic kind.

But let's forget all of this, you don't need my advice. This brings me peace. You've been doing it right all along, haven't you, without my fleeting prayers.

~

I am sitting in the same spot, glancing over the same wall art, when Deborah comes back out into the waiting room. She smiles at me.

Back home, I am sitting in the same spot I was when Deb first told me that she was pregnant. She's next to me. She thanks me for driving her today.

"I just really needed a friend," she says with a sniff.

I look at her—her tatty hair, her crossed ankles, her manicured fingers, pink, a cup of warm milk in her hand. I see me from back then—the dried blood, the spinning head, the trembling lip, and the shivers on the bus ride home. I want to tell that girl that it's okay. It's alright. Of course that day is still with her. It was a lot. She'll get past this. It's what we do.

Chapter Twenty-Nine: Evie

Today, out of all days, you should be here. You should know who I am. I wonder, do you need reminding of today?

I've decided to become an insomniac. I roll my tumbled stone back and forth against my knuckle, a lucky little Tiger Eye rock with smooth edges a kind nurse gave to me once.

I bike a bunch. I get bored. I wonder what else there is to it, this not sleeping thing. More than mindlessly sitting by the window, watching the night sky until all the stars blend and look like the same, boring single light. This seems so similar to an epiphany, this borderline breaking point.

Mostly, I wonder where you are right now. What you are doing. Who you are with.

My stationary bike broke. Already. One of the pedals got stuck mid cycle and I can't for the life of me figure out why.

That's why I end up here, at the daycare center. All I can think of is that new rock climbing wall.

A buzzing overtakes me—an internal buzzing, a kind that is energized. It makes my limbs all jittery, my eyes feel as if they are twinkling. It is like the bike, but more.

Constant. So constant of a buzz that my thoughts, my always going and going and going logical thoughts, they turn off for a moment as I dig for the staff badge inside of my purse.

Through the back gate that's always active to the staff badge, up the stairs, turn the corner, turn on the lights. The rock climbing wall is polished and smelling of rubber and stucco paint and has never been climbed before. The room itself is messy, still recovering from construction. There are cardboard boxes, tools, empty buckets everywhere. There's an old glass coffee table tucked in the corner someone must have brought in to help manage all the mess. There are stacks of paperwork covering its surface. I pull the table over to the rock climbing wall to use it as a stepping stool.

Running my fingers over the colored stubs, yellow to red to blue and green—cool and a little scratchy and inviting.

What do the colors mean? I pick the light blue simply because I like the look of it and get going. Up, up, up—I think to look down a total of four times but decide against it during each one of them. Height is not what I'm here for.

I'm not crawling, I'm climbing away, above it all, just for a moment. I want to fly. Feel my feet curl below me and my unevenness melt away. How nice it is to feel removed, knowing it is just for a moment, not needing to belong anywhere.

It feels like minutes and then it feels like hours when my trusted light blue nuggets holding me up stretch farther and farther apart from one another, making me reach and pull in ways my muscles don't like anymore.

But the buzzing doesn't care. It keeps going and going, like a soundtrack in my head, and I don't care to think much about anything else but the corner above me where the rough brown wall that claims it is a rock and the blank white canvas of a ceiling intimately meet one another. Grazing fingers, rubbing nose to nose between kisses—I think that is what they are doing up there.

When my left foot slips, my hands are the part of my body to panic. There is nothing as scary as grasping at air when you are about to fall. Slipping, slipping, I think for a moment that I may be watching myself go.

I tell myself that it is not too late, but I'm not sure for what I mean. To catch myself? For you and me? For the first time since the truth came out, I feel fine about the phrase, *you and me*.

It doesn't matter, though, because I am wrong. When I see the glass beneath me, coming closer and closer, it is too late.

I wonder, do you remember that today is my birthday?

They say if they found me earlier, if I told someone where I was going, if I bled less, it could have been an easier fix. If the glass cuts didn't sting so much, I wouldn't be screaming on the inside, if I could just open my eyes, I could find out if anyone could hear me on the outside.

I look for the buzz. It's still here with me, inside, but it is fading, fading quickly.

Chapter Thirty: Charlotte

I show up at Ben's door after the police run in. Well, really, what happened was the officer let me go with a warning and asked me to say hi to Ben for her. He rolls his eyes at me when I tell him I namedropped with a cop. When I tell him, *no, it wasn't for speeding*, he lets me in.

He waves my abrupt thank you away as we settled on the couches in his living room. He offers me coffee, or tea, and all of the nice, polite things you're supposed to do with a random acquaintance.

I apologize for yelling and pushing him away like that the last time we saw each other. Then, I apologize for pushing him away and running all those years ago.

That was it. No tearful *I still love you*s / *Darling, I'm so glad you said something / I love you too*s.

Instead, he says nothing.

I try again. "You're right," I say. "I was never truthful with you and that was wrong of me. So wrong. You didn't deserve to have your heart broken."

"Most people don't," says Ben.

"I have a *past*."

"No? You?" Ben responds sarcastically.

"This is serious," I say. He nods an apology and I know to continue. "When I was a kid—sixteen—I got pregnant. We never even talked about not keeping it, my high school boyfriend and I. We kept it from our parents in the beginning, but you know, I was always raised against it. So was he. Towards the end, he lost interest in me. I thought if only I could get everything back to the way things were before—before I got pregnant—everything would be fixed and back to normal. Then he'd stay with me."

"So, you—"

"Yes, I got an abortion."

"Okay—"

"Back-alley."

"What? How?"

"Salt saline."

"Jesus. Ok. I had no idea that was still being done." He scratches his head. "I would have been able to see where you were coming from, Charlotte. I know you were probably still wrestling with it yourself, but you must have known that about me, even back then."

"The abortion didn't happen. I mean, it did, but it didn't work. The baby survived. A little girl."

Silent again. Ben stares at me. He runs his hands through his hair. There's nothing but his breath for a while. "Shit. Where is she?" Ben finally asks.

"We were working with an agency that promotes local adoptions."

Ben nods. That seems like enough. For the first time today he touches me, squeezes my hand. We lean in close to each other, erasing the space between us. We're kissing and I slip into his lap. He carries me to the bedroom and we finally make love.

"Do you ever want to meet her?" he asks me eventually.

"Sure. Always. But also never," I say. I shrug into his bedsheets, draped around the both of us as we lay in bed for a while. "It's hard to know what would happen if I did just appear out of nowhere. I think I always assumed she didn't even know about me."

"You mean you think her family never told her that she was adopted?"

"I wouldn't. Not knowing what happened to her. Would you?"

"Maybe they don't know," says Ben.

"It's possible," I respond. I choose my next words slowly. "I think I might ruin something if I show up. I don't know what, you see, that's what I mean. By complicated. I don't know anything about her life, so it seems that if I just show up out of nowhere, there's a chance something could really change for her. And that seems risky. Does that make sense? It sounds crazy," I answer myself. "Assuming the worst for someone else and making decisions for them, for someone I don't even really know. But I just know this, Ben, I don't know how, but I do. I know I can't risk this, finding out about this hypothetical situation. Even if it drives me crazy not to."

"Sure it makes sense," says Ben. "That's how I am with Ian."

Now Ben and I just look at each other. *Really?* I want to ask. Totally clueless. *Really, is this what parents do, everyday? This is what it's like for people?* He nods into the silence.

"So this is why," Ben says. "You never wanted kids?"

I nod.

"What about now?"

"Now I'm tired of skirting around my life."

"Well thank God for that," says Ben, and kisses me on the forehead. "What are you going to do?"

"I'm going to become a lawyer. Save up to get my own place. I'm going to spend more time talking to my mother on the phone, and getting lunch with her whenever I can see her. I'm going to try to be better…at everything."

We spend the rest of the afternoon watching television and holding each other. It's nice. It's been a long time. I smile at how easy it is to pick things back up. *No,* I correct myself. *That's not what we're doing, picking up where we left off. We'll be better than we were before. We already are.*

When it starts to get dark out, we say our goodbyes and make plans to cook dinner together later in the week.

"One more thing. You need to stop stalking her," says Ben. "Even if it's only with your imagination."

I start to scoff and roll my eyes, but Ben's not smiling. He's just looking at me kindly.

"I know. I know that you're right," I respond. "One more thing," I add.

"Oh boy. What is it?"

"Will you go steady with me?" I bat my eyes at Ben.

Ben laughs and pushes me playfully out the door.

"Alright, kid," he says back.

"Don't call me that anymore."

"I know, I know. You're all grown up now." He raises his eyebrows. "It's about time."

I skip to my car, smiling at the both of us. The cloudless sky and distance mountain views whizzing by me during the drive home look much clearer than they have for a long time now.

Chapter Thirty-One: Evie

Stop asking questions, I've forgotten how to answer.

What happened? Evie. Evie. Open your eyes, Evie. Oh my God. Oh my God.

I am shaking. Is this someone else's doing, or am I shaking all by myself?

Open your eyes. I'm trying. *Open your eyes.* Fine.

Yellow foam insides of a ripped up red cushion, a single beam of white light, people, so many of them, an ambulance truck, we're outside—what am I looking at?

Evie. Oh, thank God.

I think it's Mitchell. And the building manager. And a woman. I don't know her. She's shining a light at my pupils out of one of those things doctors use to check your ears.

"What happened?" I ask.

"Evie! Jeez, Evie. You really gave us all a heart attack. What were you doing up there, so late, all alone?" It's Mitchell.

Someone is telling Mitchell to back up now.

"Do you feel dizzy at all?" The woman's face clouds my vision. She has a sharp chin. "Any sudden pain? Difficulty moving?"

Stupid questions. And nobody is answering mine. "What happened?"

"You took quite a fall," says Sharp Chin. I hear voices in the background. *Isn't it good*, someone wants to know, *that she's awake now?*

The rest of what Sharp Chin says comes to me in phrases:

Need a bit of oxygen.

Lots of blood.

A couple bruises on your legs, too.

Good thing. Manager found you and called right away.

Good thing.

~

What do you think the end feels like? I've heard it's nothing like sleep at all. I heard you wake up and lose your voice, and just kind of float there as every limb in your body takes its turn shutting itself off. I've heard you choke and forget how to breathe before your conscious goes. I've heard it's a long and dozy thing, dying.

I bet your heart paces and you feel like you're sweating, you get so scared. I bet it's terrifying, and thrilling, and peculiar, being inside of yourself yet watching yourself go further than ever before. I bet it is winter's crisp, and summer's glimmer skipping across the rear-view mirror, and nothing in between.

My teachers in grade school always told me that I think about the end too much. It's probably true.

Hannah nodded when I told her they said that. *Too intense, that Evie.*

I used to rattle off facts about death rituals at sea. I can see how that can be unnerving, a creepy little kid obsessed with wildlife funerals.

For example, adult dolphins use their heads and backs to hold up a calf who has recently died, usually for about thirty minutes before giving them up to the ocean. Magpies hold funerals, gently pecking at a dead bird, covering the body with some grass and leaves before saying goodbye.

Humans don't think about it much until it's too late, how we'd like to go. It's considered strange if we do. It's considered dark, depressing.

I know I lost a lot of blood. My blood is rare. It's usually not a problem. *But she's lost so much blood,* I hear them say. *Let's hope for the best,* they say. They think I can't hear them. I've heard it all, many times, I'm not shaken by it.

~

When I regain my consciousness, I know exactly where I am. One of the nurses even looks familiar. I feel like I've known her for my entire life and this hospital room is all mine. How else do I instinctively know there is a window to my left and a small nightstand to my right?

Hannah and Mitchell are there, and I try to remember the last time the three of us were in a room. Just the three of us.

"Do you remember anything?" Mitchell asks.

"A candle."

"Yeah. That was from me," he says and chuckles. He points to an empty takeout box. "Happy belated Birthday. From all of us. It was my idea, though. I'm also the asshole who ate the whole damn cupcake before you even woke up."

I don't remember waking up earlier. But it must be so.

"We were so busy with Hannah's surgery," he continues. "We never got to celebrate."

"I'm sorry for being a jerk," I say. "In case I didn't say it the last time I woke up." I look around the room. "Your girl seems nice. And you seem happy. *Normal*."

We both roll our eyes and laugh at that.

He leaves me alone then to rest my eyes where I lay in the hospital bed. Sleep doesn't appeal to me, though. I allow my eyes to rest outside my window on the pink and white flowers of a magnolia tree.

It's only when I feel the cool touch of paper against my chest that I realize we were never alone, just the three of us, at all. A man with curly hair stands over me, grinning. He tells me he was part of the nursing staff that got me in here and ready for a blood donation, then surgery.

"You kept mumbling about that thing while you were still in the stretcher, wouldn't let any of us rest until you had it in your arms. It was in your purse. Wanted to return it to you before I head home," he waves the bag at me, and puts it down in the empty chair near my bed. "You knocked out pretty much the second you got it in your hands, though."

It's the Mary Poppins filing folder. It's been so long since I hovered over that thing, I forgot I still had it this entire time, waiting in my purse.

"You were clutching it so tightly, I barely got you away from it in time for surgery." His orange curls wiggle as he jogs his head back and forth with his fast speech. He has a couple of smears of gray blue and purple oil paint on the beige jacket he wears over his scrubs and the only thing I can really recall about him is someone humming to French music on the radio on my way over here. Perhaps it was him.

"You know what's funny? I was just talking to a buddy of mine about what we would pull out of our homes in case of a fire or some disaster like that the other day," he says. "And I couldn't get over how tough that question actually is. Like, at first, I couldn't pick just one or two things, but then I ended up not wanting to save anything if it meant I might run out of time." He points at the folder. "I guess that's your answer."

He leaves me and Hannah to an empty room. Neither of us speak. I'm so confused.

I open up the folder, and the weirdest thing of all happens. That news clip I thought I left at the Rileys is in there, too. And it's not torn up at the edges, at all. It's perfectly intact.

~

Recovery will take a few more days. I'm a little out of it, but I'm doing well.

Mitchell keeps trying to talk about you. He thinks he's seen you, in Hannah's home, or something along those lines. Is it true? Did you come looking for me, after all, after all these years?

I want to ask Hannah, who stared at the news clipping with the same bewildered look I had earlier that day when my things were returned to me. But when I finally wake to her alone at my bedside, she is the one who does the talking this time.

"I'm sorry that I didn't believe in you," Hannah says, in her always even, but never this quiet, voice. "That you could swim."

"What are you talking about?" I ask.

"When I only let you swim on the rug instead of in the water like all the other kids," she finishes. "I was only trying to protect you. Only I had no idea how."

Hannah, my not-quite-a-mother guardian. But still, the Hannah who watched me grow up when nobody else really bothered to. *We were lucky*, we'd always say.

I want to tell her how she was always a part-time participant in my life, and how it drove me crazy. I didn't think it was fair.

Only now do I know that we're all part-timers, no matter what. All we have for always is our minds, our palms, our toes, our memories. Sometimes all those go, too. But it's okay, I think. That's what makes it all so precious.

I look at her and just smile. "Hannah. You've done more than enough," I say and squeeze her hand in a tender way that makes her stir. "You've really outdone yourself."

Hannah nods gratefully, with the smallest tears in her eyes, and agrees to go home and get some rest.

Chapter Thirty-Two: Charlotte

She comes in six times to get her blood drawn, once a month for half a year. I only volunteer in the early mornings, four hours a week, before my classes and my shift at the travel agency begin. But she always seemed to know that I am watching, wanting to know, holding my breath with her. Her schedule always lines up with the days that I am there.

I am in one of the back rooms with a new client, giving her various pages of our informational kits. Soft-toned, big-eyed, and sharp posture, we sit there just the two of us. I like this new client and am happy when she tells me that this is all very helpful, even if she only says it to be kind and polite. She smiles when I give her one of the take-home packets we always have on hand, full of vaccination info and free condoms. I notice that we are low and make a mental note to put together a few more before leaving for the day.

After setting her up with one of our medical examiners to talk about getting on the birth control pill, I see Once-A-Month, nervous and waiting for her STD results. A man I've never seen before with cheerfully wrinkled eyes comes in with her today. He places one of his heavy arms around her shoulders and she looks calmer.

"It's a wonderful day for a miracle, isn't it?" he says to me back in the waiting room after I walk Once-A-Month to her chair.

The first time Once-A-Month came in, she told me about her ex-boyfriend. How they dated happily for five months before she found out that he was a sex addict. *A real one*, she had said with an eye roll. How she walked in on him cheating on her one day, and how his ex-girlfriend found her on Facebook and told her everything. How he eventually admitted it and said there had been plenty this whole time, more than he could count. How he was sick before, but was better now, he guessed.

She got tested for everything we could think of that first time she came in, and they all came out fine. She still wasn't at rest. Once a month, she'd come in and we'd run the same tests all over again. *How many until we can be completely sure?* she asked one day, itching at her skin after the needle prick as if she could scratch away anything inside of her that was no-good. We told her once was fine. She didn't believe us.

I'm not sure if someone finally told her something other than *you're fine*, or if it was a number she calculated all by herself, but soon everyone knew it was six months for Once-A-Month. Only then would she be at ease.

I'm so mad at myself for being so stupid, she had said to me. How much I wanted to tell her how often I hear that here, and I hate hearing it every time. There's nothing stupid about searching for love, even if that love is just a love for our own bodies. There's nothing stupid about needing help sometimes, or just some new wisdom we tuck away for a later time. Instead I say nothing and offer her a comforting smile. It's taken me years and years of running, and loving, and hating, to understand. If it takes her six months, that isn't so bad.

I like volunteering at *Planned Parenthood*. It makes me feel useful. Like I'm really good at turning nothing good into something great. And even on the days that are slow or grueling, at least there's the comfort I've developed around the medical staff, no longer pacing or avoiding anything that looks like a medical facility. I even went in for an annual physical a week ago, overdue for longer than I care to admit.

Once-A-Month's last test comes in today. When she receives the negative results, she cries. She runs past the front desk and the scattered cubicles to the back room where I still sit, shifting through old brochures. We hug for what seemed like ages and laugh with tears in our eyes.

~

It's been less than a year since Mom left the country and I am not a bit surprised at how settled in she is already. She's a regular at the local yoga studio. She has a meditation routine already— always by the fountain outside the studio apartment that she is renting for herself, so she can hear the water gather gently behind her in between breaths with her eyes closed. She's taking a cooking class to eat as the Austrians do, and she travels by train all of the time. *The grocer likes me*, she tells me over the phone.

I tell her about volunteering at *Planned Parenthood*. I tell her about the people we help. I told her about Once-a-Month before. She doesn't ask about you. All I tell her about all of that is that it isn't right, me interfering with a decision made and done with long ago. She is patient, as experienced mothers tend to be.

I knew the folded-up paper she handed to me had to do with you the minute it was in my hands. Maybe that's why when all I saw were some words of well wishes and an address without an explanation, I followed it blindly, driving fifty-seven minutes and knocking on the front door confidently instead of laying out my options in the car for the next twenty minutes the way I might have done so many years ago. Hell, so many weeks ago.

In retrospect, I should have known. The neat pile of checks made out to Hannah Mission held together with a single paperclip, tucked away in my father's top desk drawer. I didn't think much of it. Finances such as these were something we began shifting through right after his funeral and finished up gathering when we put the house on the market. When mother and I were packing, we gathered everything from that desk drawer in handfuls, stuffed it into a manila folder and tossed it into a box. It was long forgotten, at least by me.

All the things sitting in storage for a while—old ski clothes, schoolbooks, and such—I figured it was all going to the trash or to charity once I got around to it. The paperwork, I was planning to shred.

But the note she gave me with this mysterious address got me thinking. From the airport, I hurried back to my new apartment, carrying in one of the storage boxes full of forgotten things high over my head. Once I found that check, I unfolded the piece of paper my mother gave me like a mad woman and desperately hoped this Hannah woman was a sick stranger my parents took pity on. A church service project, perhaps. But who are any of us trying to fool? Sure enough, the addresses matched when I held up one of my father's check receipts to my last bucket list item.

The next day, a young couple answered the door. The woman gave him a look, but the man told her how this would be good for you, for Evie, he just knew it. It'll solve all of your issues and so on. He told me you've been in a bit of slump lately.

My shoulders dropped as I realized this may not be the best idea. I barged in here like a desperate romantic looking for her rom com ending, pounding down someone's door, not for answers, but for confessions. Knowing I have no right to roll my eyes as they tried to compartmentalize whatever it is that you're going through into the simple "slump" category, but roll my eyes I did anyhow. The man looked at me as if I am an angel. The answer to all of his prayers, the solution to all of your problems.

Sweetheart, I am anything but that.

They handed me yet another address jotted down on a piece of binder paper, folded in two. Another car ride, in fact a few. I drive around just watching out for you, but at a distance. Always at a safe distance. Just enough to see a ponytail in a sea of other brunettes, enough to see the heel of a sneaker or the cuffs of a pair of light jeans. I shouldn't take too close of a look.

~

I'm not sure how I know when I find you, the real you, walking out of your apartment building. It is one of those feelings you just don't let become a fully thought-out thought. That will somehow ruin things. At least this time I didn't just pick some random out of a crowd in front of the community college.

A wordless instinct seems to be running our lives lately. So when the ambulance shows up, outside that community daycare center I see you outside of sometimes, I just know that it's for you. I follow it. It's really late at night. Why were you out at this hour? Couldn't you sleep?

No matter what, today is a good day. I always remember today. Today is your birthday. But this year is the first year that I think it as a fully thought-out thought: Happy birthday to you.

Chapter Thirty-Three: Bennet Hill Hospital

Despite her specialty in nutritional counsel and diabetic lifestyle coaching, Nurse Deanna has a cherry coke and either an energy bar or a single packet of fruit snacks every night from her parked car minutes before work. Since starting in 2003, she's always worked the nightshift.

But today is different. She turns her back to the window. It's afternoon in California, and it's so damn bright. Today, Nurse Deanna is late to work and doesn't have time for her in-car snack ritual.

Out of a general respect for tradition, she tries to steal a few small, pleasant gulps as she walks into the building, but spills half of the cherry coke can on her uniform when a woman curled over herself bumps into her. They are both by the sliding doors at the entrance.

She's not a small woman, nor a large one. She is using her knee as a tabletop for some forms she is filling out and trying to walk at the same time when she bumps into Nurse Deanna. Cherry coke bursts all over the place. Nurse Deanna is not in a good mood.

After dabbing at her uniform with a paper towel and some sink water, Nurse Deanna returns to the front desk and shifts through today's files, taking her time, especially as she scans for any updates on the names she recognizes. Her returning patients.

Because her load is light today—not unusual given the reason she was removed from her usual shift is that they were running low on patients anyhow—it's expected for Nurse Deanna to help support the blood donation department. Something she usually enjoys. Because this blood donation station runs from the hospital itself 24/7, there are always donors trickling in from Bennet Hill Hospital for patients in need of blood transfusions.

Nurse Deanna checks in, nods hello to the two other nurses on duty today, washes her hands, and grabs a folder. She calls out a name, turns and trusts the patient is following her to the first donation station on the right-hand side.

When the donation room, or any room in the hospital for that matter, is nearly empty, shifts go by much slower. She thinks nearly everyone in the medical industry secretly loves a little drama, a little rush.

But today is a slow day. The kind of day when words even sound softer and lazier. Nurse Deanna wonders if it's that, or if it's the absence of the sugar boost she's become so disgustingly dependent on, that is causing her to yawn so much already. She turns and sure enough, her patient is sitting with her sleeve already rolled up. She is red-handed, literally. Nurse Deanna sees she has not washed off the spilt cherry coke from her fingers. The smell hits her before anything else.

Cherry Fingers has dainty wrists and small veins. Small enough for a butterfly needle, which Nurse Deanna threads and secures into the holder with a sheath. She verifies the blood collection tube with the patient, and notices that she herself is in need of a new manicure. Her chipped dark purple thumb removes a disinfectant wipe from the dispenser on the wall. She usually goes for the same violet blue, but went for a "younger" dark purple this time at the recommendation of her nail lady, because everything should be done in moderation, including change and spontaneity. They even teach you that in nursing school.

There is always one lesson that stands out much clearer than the rest during a prolonged schooling or training of some sort. A moment where for no reason at all, one is most sharp and facts learned during this moment just cling. For Nurse Deanna, during nursing school, it was the image that came to mind when she was first taught how to disinfect properly. Using a circular motion, wax-on-wax-off if you will, to avoid dragging the wipe over the same piece of skin twice. Now every time, she thinks of Karate Kid.

Disinfected and pricked, the blood begins to rush. Nurse Deanna watches as it bounces off the collection tube walls and settles. She is a rare blood type, Nurse Deanna notices as she reads the label on the blood collection tube and waits for it to fill.

The power of small talk is another topic they sometimes emphasize during nursing school, but Nurse Deanna was no longer in an extra sharp focus mode for that lesson. Safe topics include: weekend plans, family members who are present or you saw in the waiting room, jobs and daily responsibilities.

Cherry Fingers doesn't have a ring on her finger, but neither does Nurse Deanna and she believes she is significantly older than her patient. She decides to ask Cherry Fingers about her weekend plans since she looks nervous, and Nurse Deanna can't hold that damn soda and energy bar that she shouldn't be eating anyway against this poor woman forever.

But Cherry Fingers doesn't respond, goes on looking forward at an old painting of a mountain in faded colors that looks like the kind of artwork made for a standard living room set in the seventies.

Anyway, Cherry Fingers must not have heard her. People are constantly telling Nurse Deanna her voice is too soft and she must learn to project. Especially when working the waiting rooms and when attending dinner parties with longer tables or louder elbow neighbors.

After sixty seconds or so, Nurse Deanna removes the needle and instructs Cherry Finger to apply pressure with the cotton ball as she wraps her arm. Cherry Fingers smiles and nods her head.

Just then Donald rushes in. He's a nurse's assistant that started at Bennet Hill Hospital three years ago, a year after Nurse Deanna did. He has instructions from the second floor, and no one was answering the front desk. Slow days.

"How are you feeling? Any dizziness, nausea?" Nurse Deanna asks her patient after sending Donald away.

"No," says Cherry Fingers. "I feel fine. Thank you." There is a paleness to her, but a peculiar one, not a sickly one, Nurse Deanna notices. It's been this way since she walked through the doors. Some people just have naturally ghostly complexions, so different from Nurse Deanna's year-round tan and her cheeks that always look a little flustered.

"It is not custom to meet a patient when donating," starts Nurse Deanna slowly. Confidentiality laws typically keep blood donors and their recipients from ever knowing who each other are. It was an odd message from Donald. "But one of the family members is eager to express his gratitude and requested it. Says he knows you, but didn't know your blood type. Knew your name and everything. He's grateful. So, anyway. Would you like to see the brother?"

"Please don't," Cherry Fingers says. Rubbing her hazel eye with the back of her free hand. Cherry Fingers says again, quieter this time, "Please don't." She looks tired.

Nurse Deanna, worried her patient is getting too light-headed from the blood loss, instructs her to bend her knees and fills a plastic cup with the apple juice they keep in a mini fridge for times like these. When she turns back with the full cup, Cherry Fingers is out of her seat.

"There is no need for that," Cherry Finger's voice trails as Nurse Deanna watches her glide through the automatic swinging door with gentle little steps. The strong wind that comes through every so often breezes through the entrance with one more gush before the automatic doors go slamming shut again. Just the same as they do every other afternoon in the blood donation department.

A few minutes pass and the wind swishes through one last time. Nurse Deanna turns to quietly curse at that damn door. It's way too windy today. She stops when Cherry Fingers is standing before her, again, smiling sweetly.

She looks calm and collected, now. Friendly. As if they were old friends. "Can I ask a favor of you?"

Nurse Deanna can't think of one good reason to say yes. But like she noticed earlier this afternoon, everything seems off about today.

Chapter Thirty-Four: Evie

"Vietnamese go by the year you were born, not what month you were born in," said Mei-Anh with a swift toss of yesterday's copy of the Los Angeles Times, the horoscope section. We both couldn't believe they still print those out.

Mei-Anh must be a new nurse here. She is always asking me kind questions she doesn't listen for the answers to. How are you doing otherwise? How are you liking the cooler weather outside? Looks like rain, doesn't it? What television shows do you like to watch? What's the first thing you're going to do when you get home?

Because Mitchell was in love and felt particularly hopeful because of it.

Because a nurse was having an off day and decided to break the rules.

Because I woke up in bed with more energy than I have had in a long time.

Because something inside of me—either my organs, or my bones, or my spirit—must have found the donated blood easier to digest than most.

Because your mother has always somehow known that this day would come and knew the exact moment when you were ready to be pushed towards it.

Because home pulled you back and I stayed local.

I've always resisted meant-to-be. But so many thoughtless moments, the moments that make up our different everyday lives, have brought us here— in this room, at this time; me, a survivor yet again, you, a savior?

I feel strong today. The doctor raises both of her eyebrows in an unamused way when I say it. That must be a line she hears all of the time, especially from hospital breakouts, like I am today.

Jumping upon the go-ahead to go home safely, I am packing up the few belongings I have here with me. Mei-Anh chuckles when she sees me looking at the perfectly intact news clip. The one about our beginning.

"What's so important about that thing, anyhow?"

"Excuse me?" I ask.

"One of those nurses, down in the blood lab. She wouldn't rest until it was in your hands. She was almost hysterical about it. You were about to go into surgery, for goodness' sake."

"The blood lab? I got a blood donation, didn't I?"

Mei-Anh nods. "Yes, she was working that day. It was really weird for her to come up here like that," she goes on. "Completely against protocol, between you and me," she says in loud whisper. She points at the news clip, then. "Must have been real important to get that to you, whatever the hell it says.

"Anyways, I asked one of the other nurses to keep it safe. He said he put it in your purse. Looks like you got it alright," Mei-Anh says.

With this new information, I turn that thing around in my hands again and again, and it is then, in the lightest shade of pencil, I see what must be your handwriting scribbled on the back.

~

Something's not right. I order a plain coffee, no whipped cream, and pick a round table for two in the back where the chalkboard menu hangs, and the roasted coffee beans smell their strongest, and the blender hums its loudest, and I take a sip from the tan paper cup, no whipped cream, and all I taste is foam.

The shop is clean and well-lighted, but I can hardly see the people sitting on the other side of the room. Doors swing. I alternate between drinking nothing to stopping for no interruptions between swallows, still no you.

You said to meet you here at noon and it is nine minutes after. Where are you?

Then there's a swish and a stomp, and there you are. You're not very graceful with entrances.

When I imagined what this moment would be like you always spoke first, or at least smiled. But you look horrified standing in front of me. You don't even sit.

You look right at me and I wonder if I should wave. Call your name out. No, that's dumb. Pull yourself together, Evie.

"Hi," you say eventually, pause, pull out your chair, blink a few times. "Evie."

My name doesn't sound like my own when you say it. Are you crying? I always thought you would, but what a selfish thing that is to ask of you. I nod so you know that you're right, it's me.

The redness of the two brims and the moistness of your insides, I can't look away, there's yellow in your eye. But not like the sun yellow. Like autumn leaves meant for falling but kept dangling in a balmy kind of warmth with a very faint wind blowing kind of yellow. Yellow that can't be yellow unless there are other colors there, and I have a funny feeling that you won't say something just for the sake of saying something, and I wouldn't say I feel a connection of any sort, but there's some kind of comfort here. Has it reached you too?

Has the tension you carried in here on the small of your back loosened, did I imagine the gap widen a bit between your shoulders and your ears?

"I know you have questions," you say. "Ask me anything."

"Did you name me?" Out of all the things I've ever wondered about you, dreamt of asking in the pretend conversations we used to have in my head, I never once wondered about this one. It's the only thing I can think of worth asking.

And your laugh isn't thunder like I thought it would be, but your eyes are an Indian summer, and that's enough for now.

Chapter Thirty-Five: Charlotte

People say that we all turn into our parents.
Eventually.

My mother is the strongest woman I know. She
volunteers endlessly, runs every day, plays tennis
every week, and always has a smile on her face. She
is a good-hearted woman, a friend, a Christian, an
optimist.

Even so, I'm terrified of becoming anything else
but me. Please understand that I had a great
example. She is the reason I am here. And yet, still.

In case it isn't obvious, I have no idea what to do
or say. I see you sitting there with your hands
clutching the bottom of your wooden chair and your
feet, leaning back on your heels, back and forth, in
your red and black rain boots. I know you are
probably angry with me. I know that it hurts.

I'm not going to sit here and pretend like this
isn't awkward. Of course, it is awkward. I don't
know you. I don't know your struggle. Maybe I
made the right decision all those years ago in some
messed up little way. I'm still sorry for it. Whoever
you have turned out to be, I hope you haven't been
fighting yourself.

Looking at you now, I believe that you are not a sunset. You are a crashing, a breaking, a roar. You're rising and setting, and everything in between. You don't believe in caution or moving around the planet with ease.

This world is mean sometimes. It keeps going after the most horrible things, it pushes, and probes, and ages us all. Sometimes it clouds you over just because. It'll swallow your light. But I'm here to tell you that none of that matters. Look at the consistency of the sun rising every morning and you'll know it is so. You are frightening, and eruptive, and I love you, believe me. I knew it since the moment I thought I'd never get to see you again.

But I see you now. You are real, and so am I.

Epilogue

Two women sit at Ernie's Café a couple strokes past noon. There is a pink tint to the window glass from the light, and all of the people crowded into the narrow, black wooden frame make the room look cozy. No one thinks of how these two women used to be strangers, and at first glance they could even be mistaken for friends catching up over a cup of coffee.

Almost. But not quite.

About The Author

Vered Hazanchuk is based in California, where she works as a public relations professional by day, closet-no-longer novelist by night. She received her degree in literature and creative writing from UC Santa Barbara's College of Creative Studies.

Let's Keep in Touch!
Follow Vered on Instagram @veredhazanchuk
Visit www.veredhazanchuk.com

Please support an independent writer with a review! Find Vered on Amazon & Goodreads.

Made in the USA
Thornton, CO
05/11/22 22:17:25

0ea99892-0a75-457a-aa7e-7060fa708fbdR01